W9-BTA-787

BINKY
UNDER PRESSURE

KIDS CAN PRESS

To Mom and Dad, for all their support and love

Text and illustrations © 2011 Ashley Spires

Kids Can Press acknowledges the financial support of the Government of Ontario, through the Ontario Media Development Corporation's Ontario Book Initiative; the Ontario Arts Council; the Canada Council for the Arts; and the Government of Canada, through the BPIDP, for our publishing activity.

Published in Canada by
Kids Can Press Ltd.
25 Dockside Drive
Toronto, ON M5A 0B5

Published in the U.S. by
Kids Can Press Ltd.
2250 Military Road
Tonawanda, NY 14150

www.kidscanpress.com

The artwork in this book was rendered in ink, watercolor, cat fur, bits of kitty litter and the occasional paw print.
The text is set in Fontoon.

Edited by Tara Walker
Series designer: Karen Powers
Designed by Rachel Di Salle and Marie Bartholomew

The hardcover edition of this book is smyth sewn casebound.
The paperback edition of this book is limp sewn with a drawn-on cover.
Manufactured in Shen Zhen, Guang Dong, P.R. China, in 4/2011 by Printplus Limited

CM 11 0 9 8 7 6 5 4 3 2 1
CM PA 11 0 9 8 7 6 5 4 3 2 1

Library and Archives Canada Cataloguing in Publication

Spires, Ashley, 1978–
          Binky under pressure / by Ashley Spires.

(A Binky adventure)
ISBN 978-1-55453-504-0 (bound). ISBN 978-1-55453-767-9 (pbk.)

I. Title. II. Series: Spires, Ashley, 1978– . Binky adventure.

PS8637.P57B555 2010   j741.5'971   C2011-901071-2

Kids Can Press is a *l'Orus*™ Entertainment company

F.U.R.S.T. IN NO WAY ENDORSES THE DISCLOSURE OF F.U.R.S.T. PROCEDURE AND PROTOCOL WITHIN THIS BOOK. THIS IS A BOOK OF FICTION AND ANY RESEMBLANCE TO ACTUAL F.U.R.S.T. POLICY IS PURELY COINCIDENTAL.

F.U.R.S.T. Felines of the Universe
Ready for Space Travel

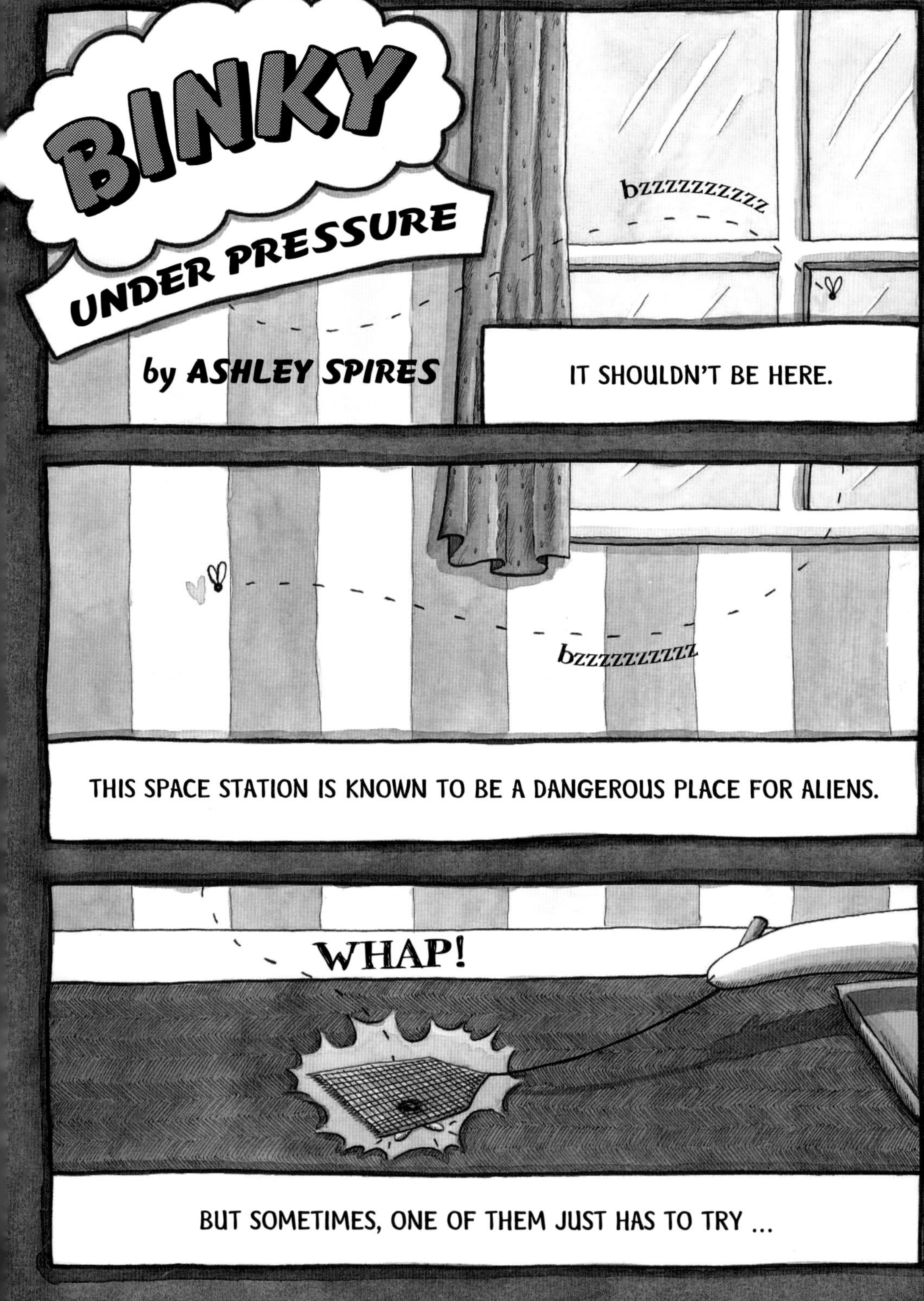
BINKY
UNDER PRESSURE
by ASHLEY SPIRES
bzzzzzzzzzz
IT SHOULDN'T BE HERE.
bzzzzzzzzzz
THIS SPACE STATION IS KNOWN TO BE A DANGEROUS PLACE FOR ALIENS.
WHAP!
BUT SOMETIMES, ONE OF THEM JUST HAS TO TRY ...

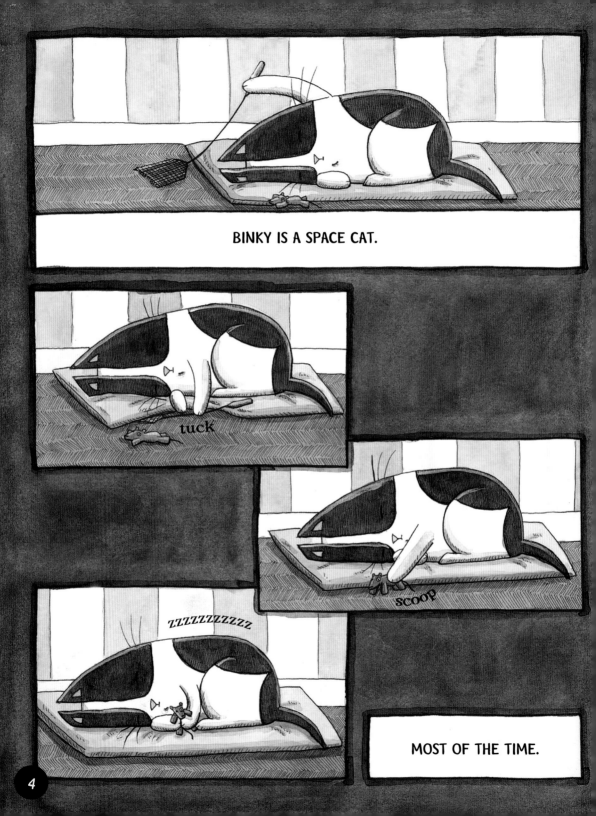

BINKY IS A SPACE CAT.

tuck

scoop

ZZZZZZZZZZZ

MOST OF THE TIME.

4

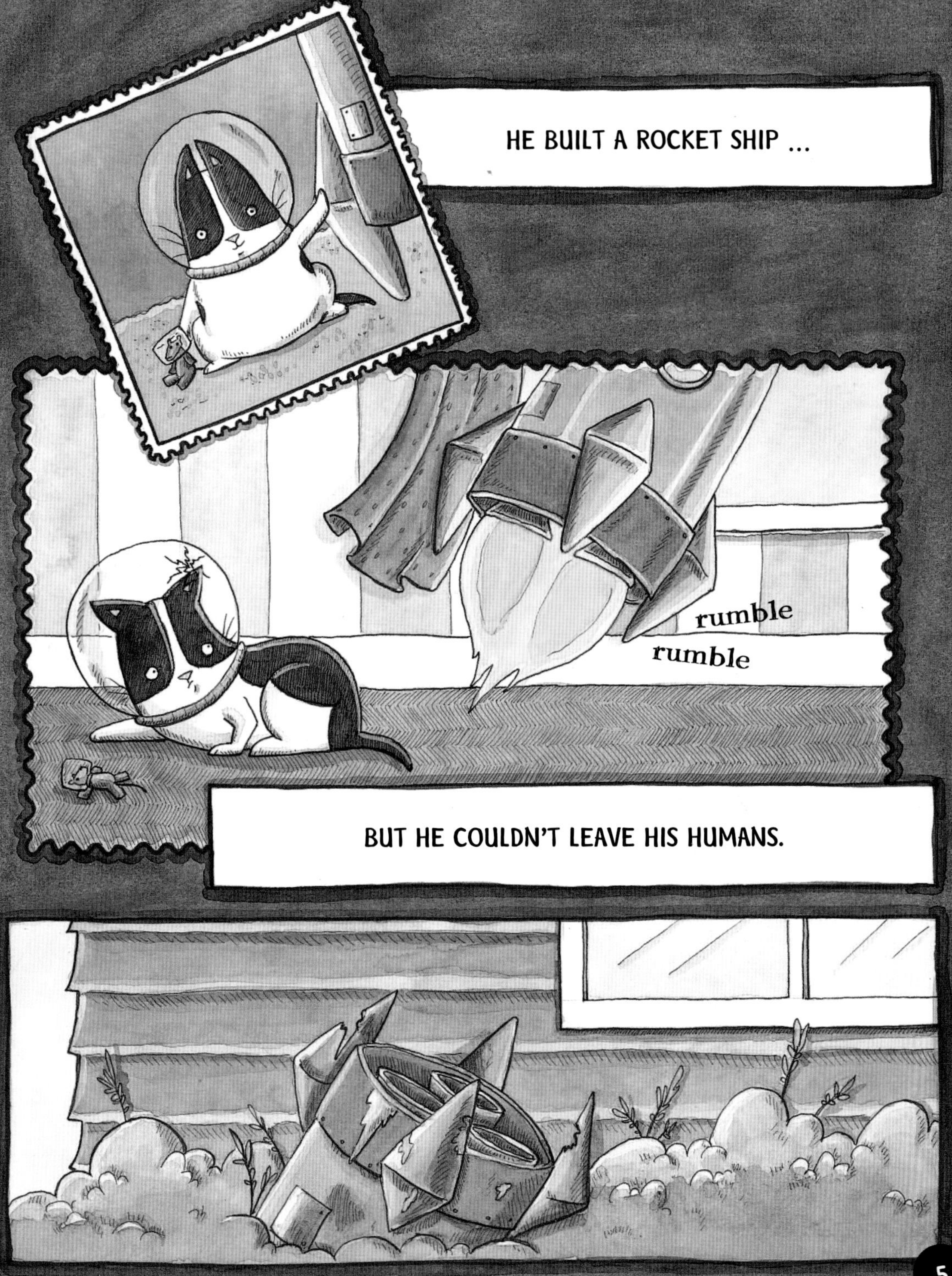
HE BUILT A ROCKET SHIP ...
rumble
rumble
BUT HE COULDN'T LEAVE HIS HUMANS.

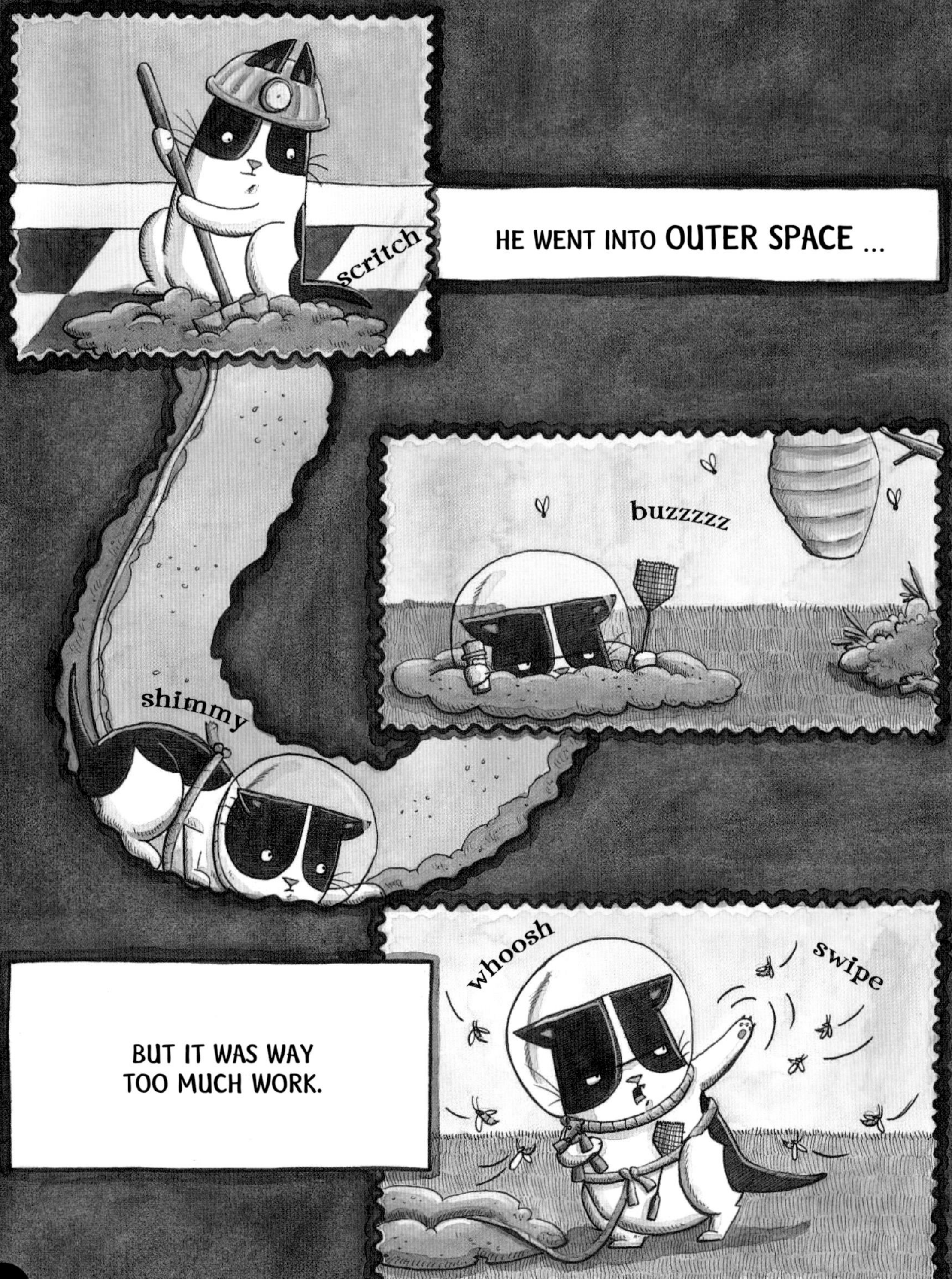
scritch
HE WENT INTO OUTER SPACE ...
shimmy
buzzzzz
whoosh
swipe
BUT IT WAS WAY TOO MUCH WORK.

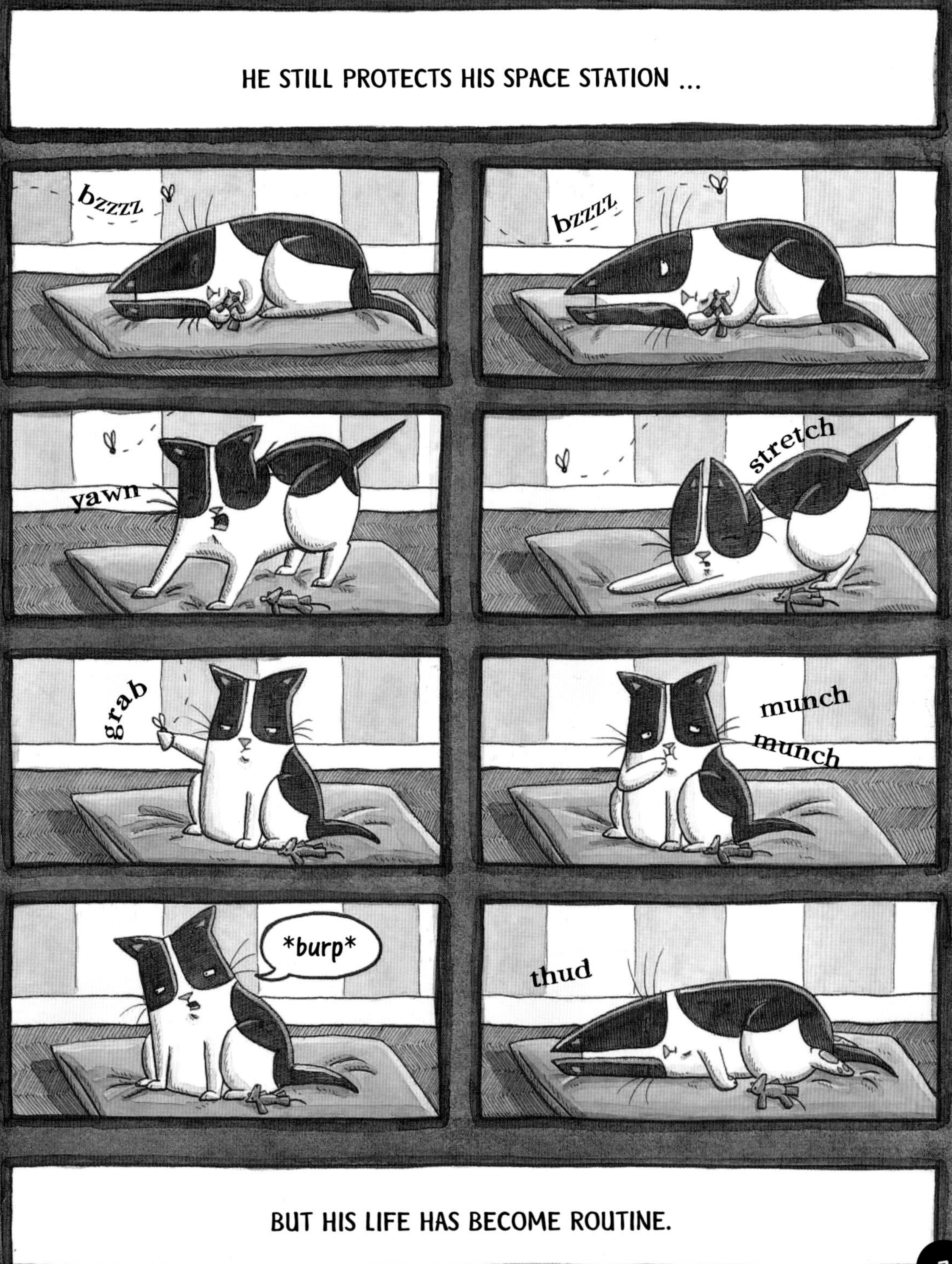
HE STILL PROTECTS HIS SPACE STATION ...
bzzzz
bzzzz
yawn
stretch
grab
munch
munch
burp
thud
BUT HIS LIFE HAS BECOME ROUTINE.

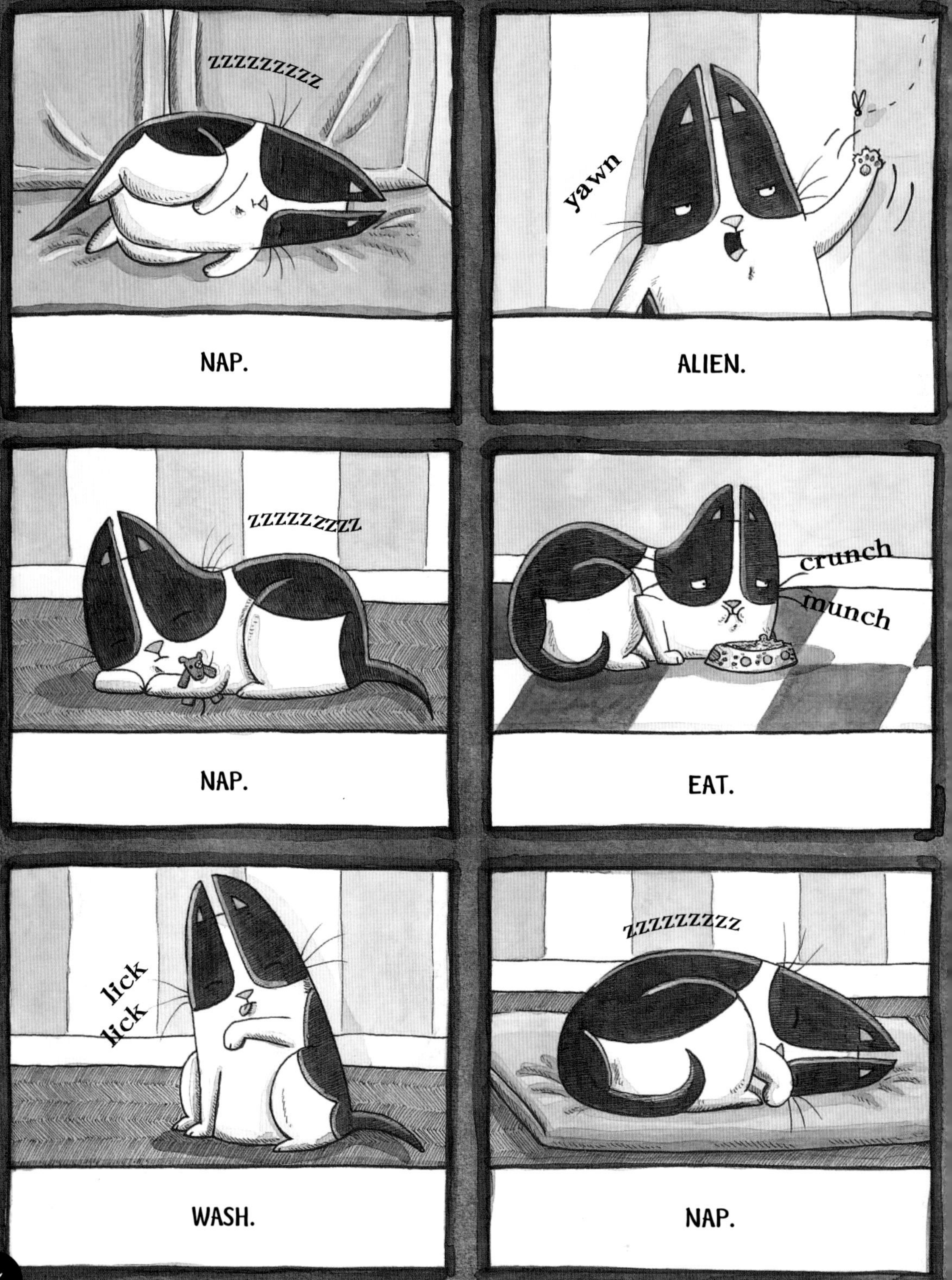
zzzzzzzzz
NAP.
yawn
ALIEN.
zzzzzzzzz
NAP.
crunch
munch
EAT.
lick
lick
WASH.
zzzzzzzzz
NAP.

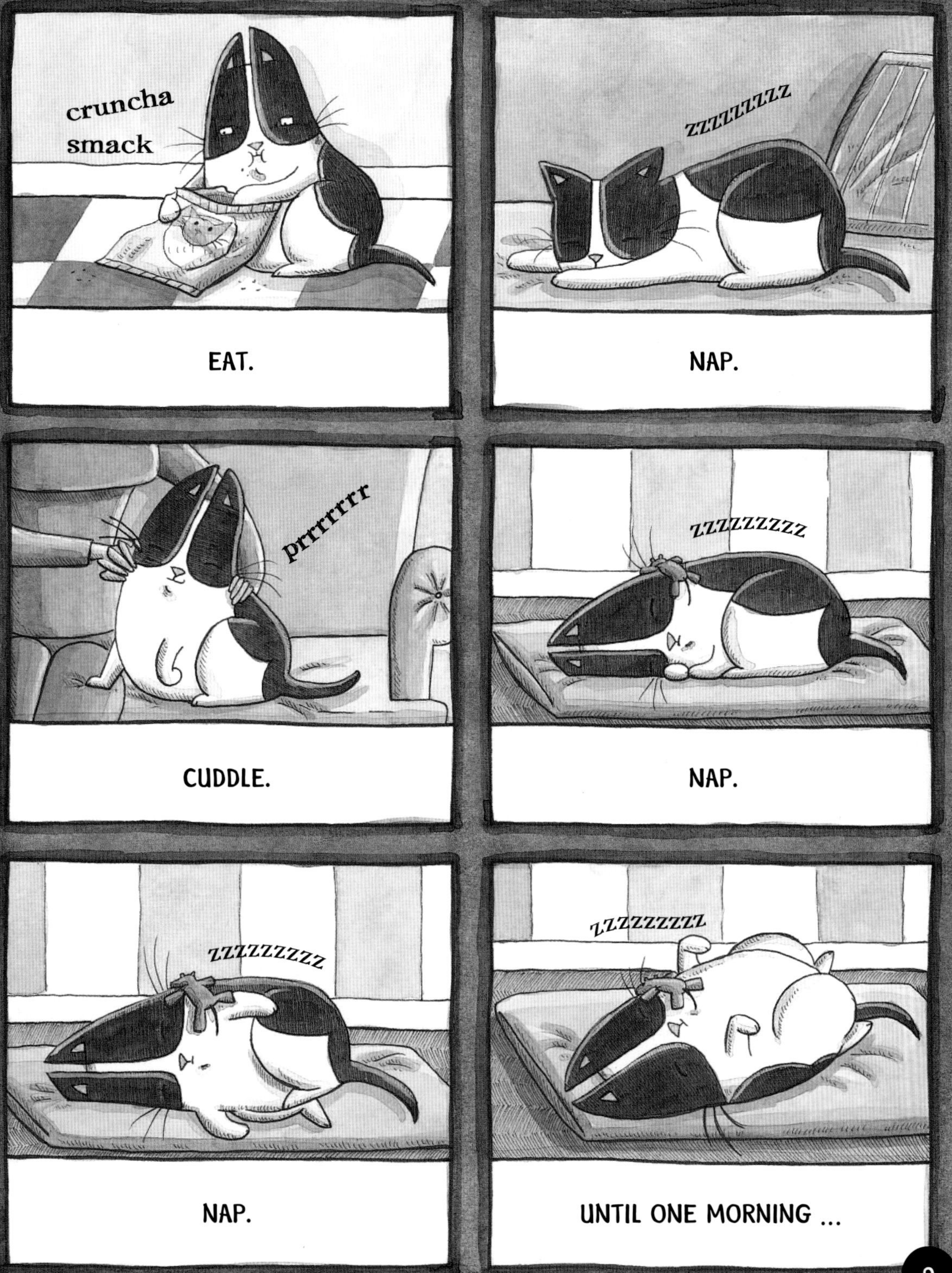

cruncha
smack
EAT.
ZZZZZZZZ
NAP.
prrrrrrr
CUDDLE.
ZZZZZZZZZ
NAP.
ZZZZZZZZZ
NAP.
ZZZZZZZZZ
UNTIL ONE MORNING ...

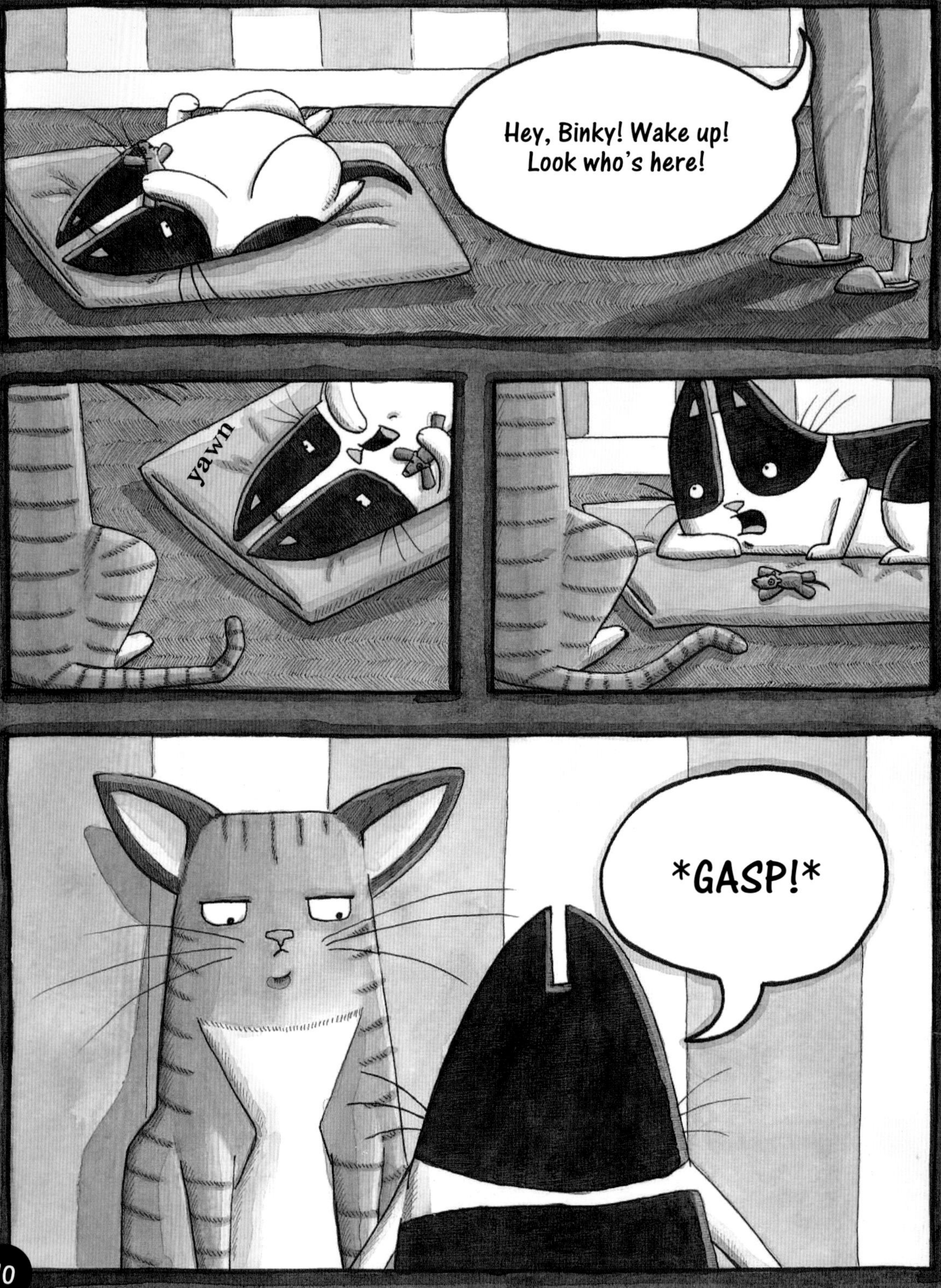
Hey, Binky! Wake up!
Look who's here!
yawn
GASP!

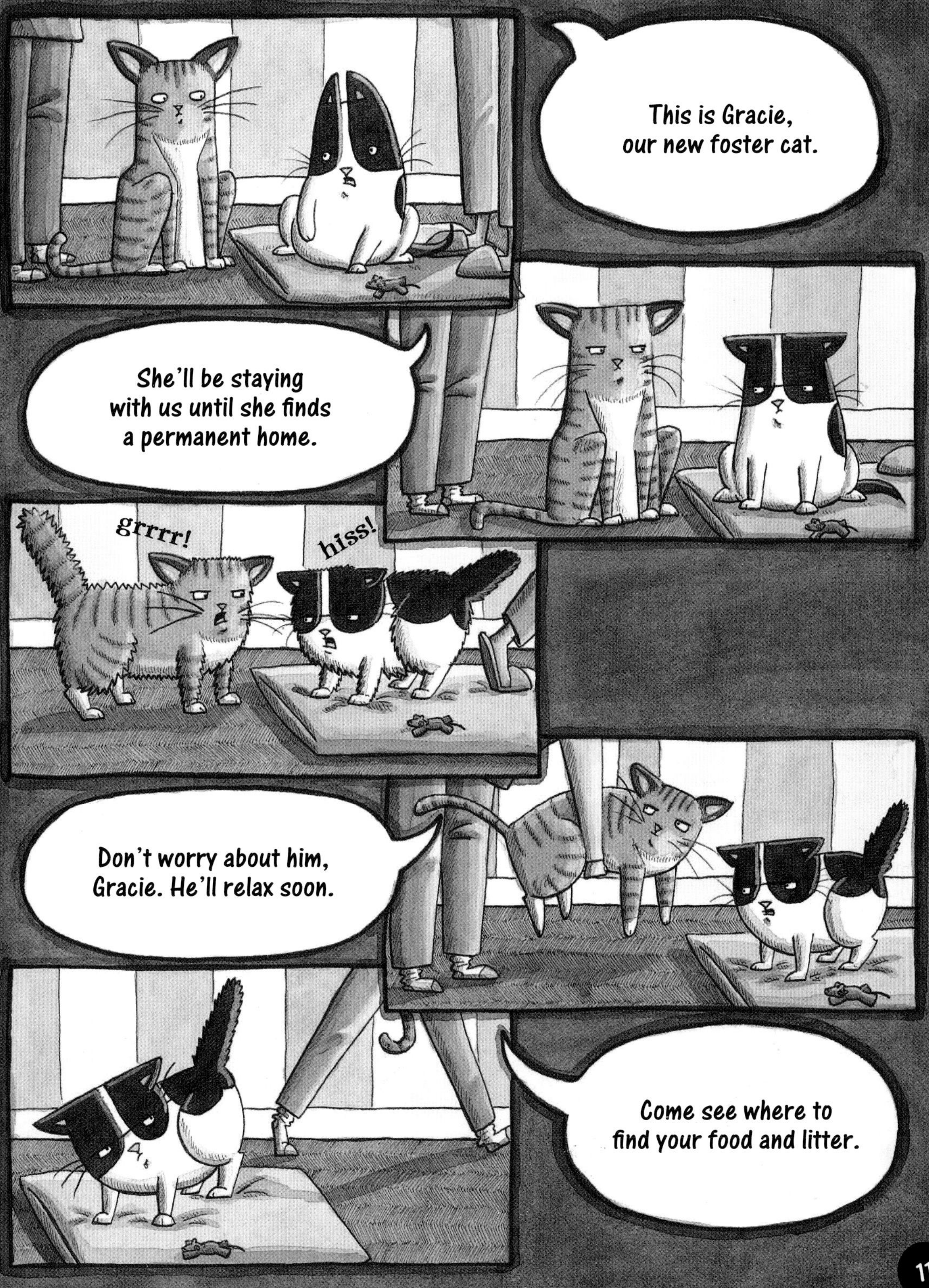
This is Gracie, our new foster cat.
She'll be staying with us until she finds a permanent home.
grrrr!
hiss!
Don't worry about him, Gracie. He'll relax soon.
Come see where to find your food and litter.

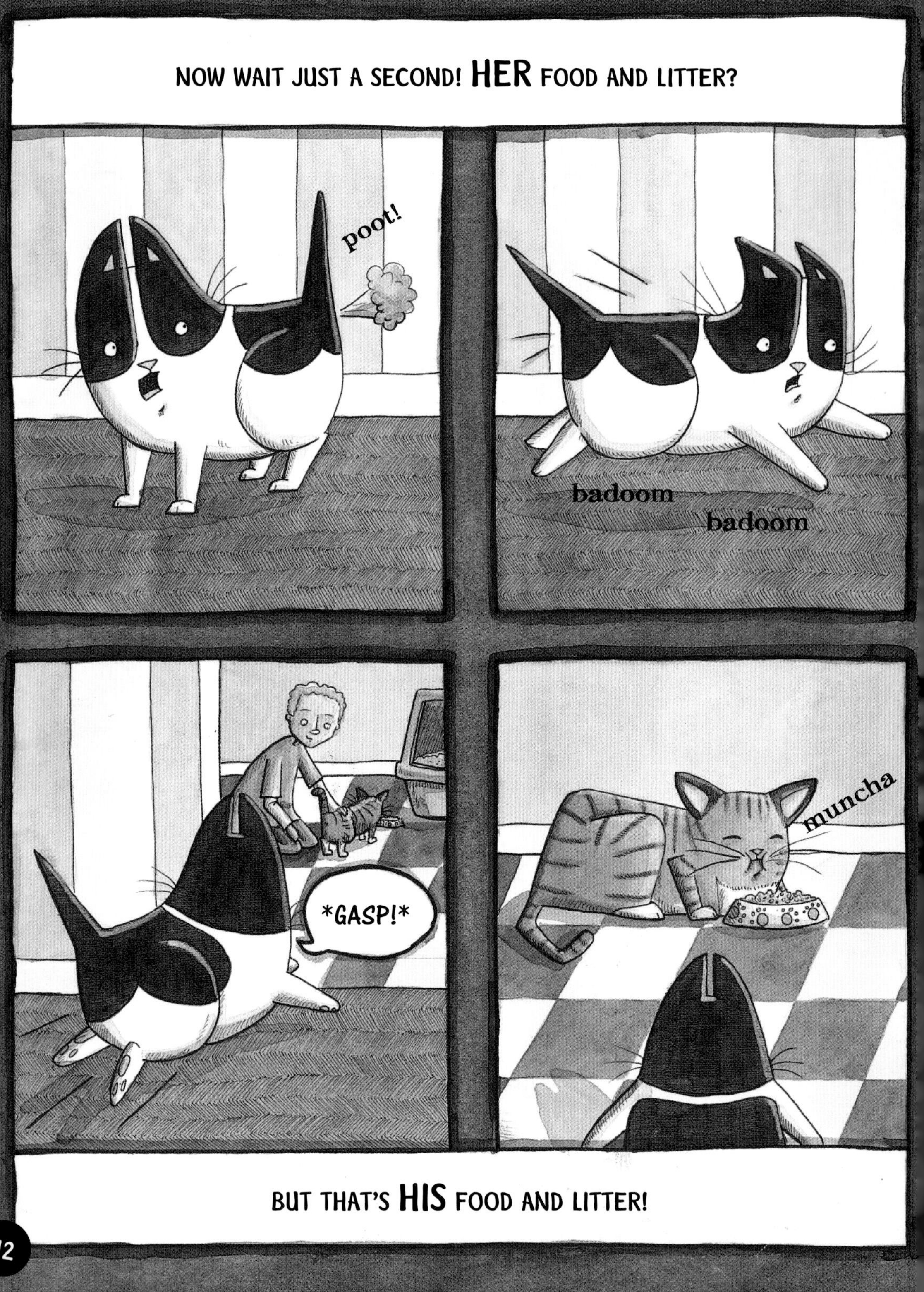
NOW WAIT JUST A SECOND! HER FOOD AND LITTER?
poot!
badoom
badoom
GASP!
muncha
BUT THAT'S HIS FOOD AND LITTER!

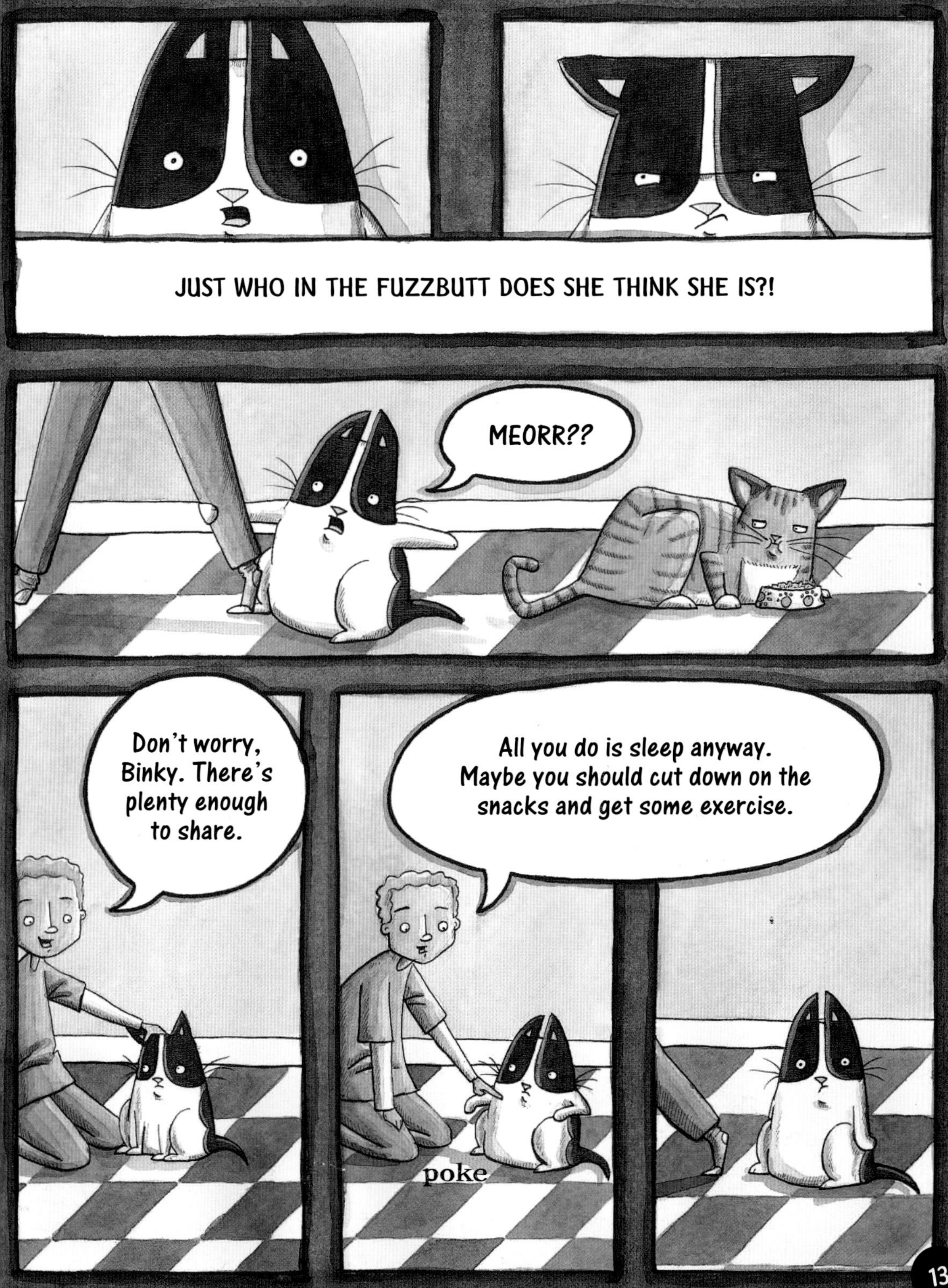
JUST WHO IN THE FUZZBUTT DOES SHE THINK SHE IS?!
MEORR??
Don't worry, Binky. There's plenty enough to share.
All you do is sleep anyway. Maybe you should cut down on the snacks and get some exercise.
poke

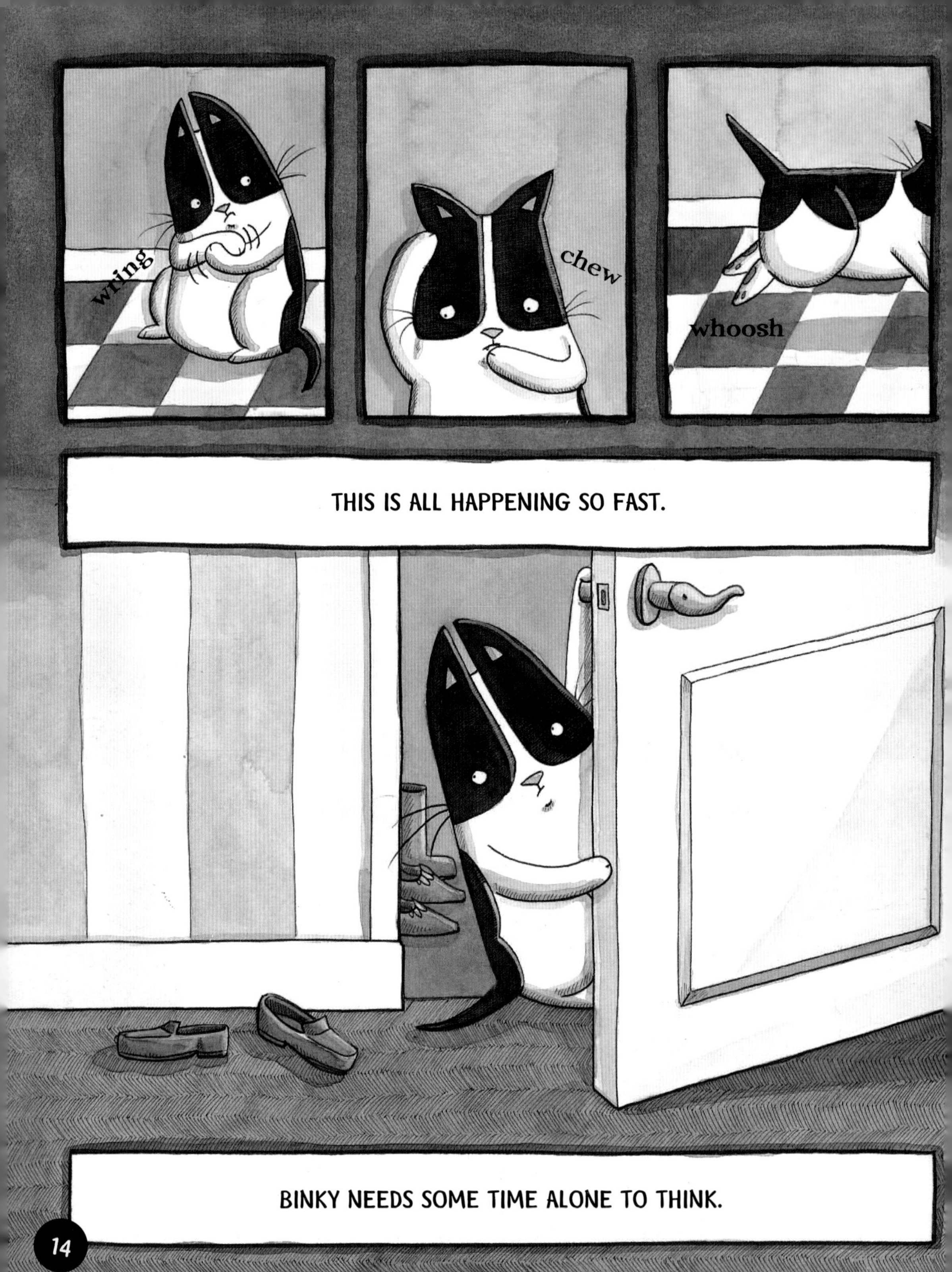
wring
chew
whoosh
THIS IS ALL HAPPENING SO FAST.
BINKY NEEDS SOME TIME ALONE TO THINK.

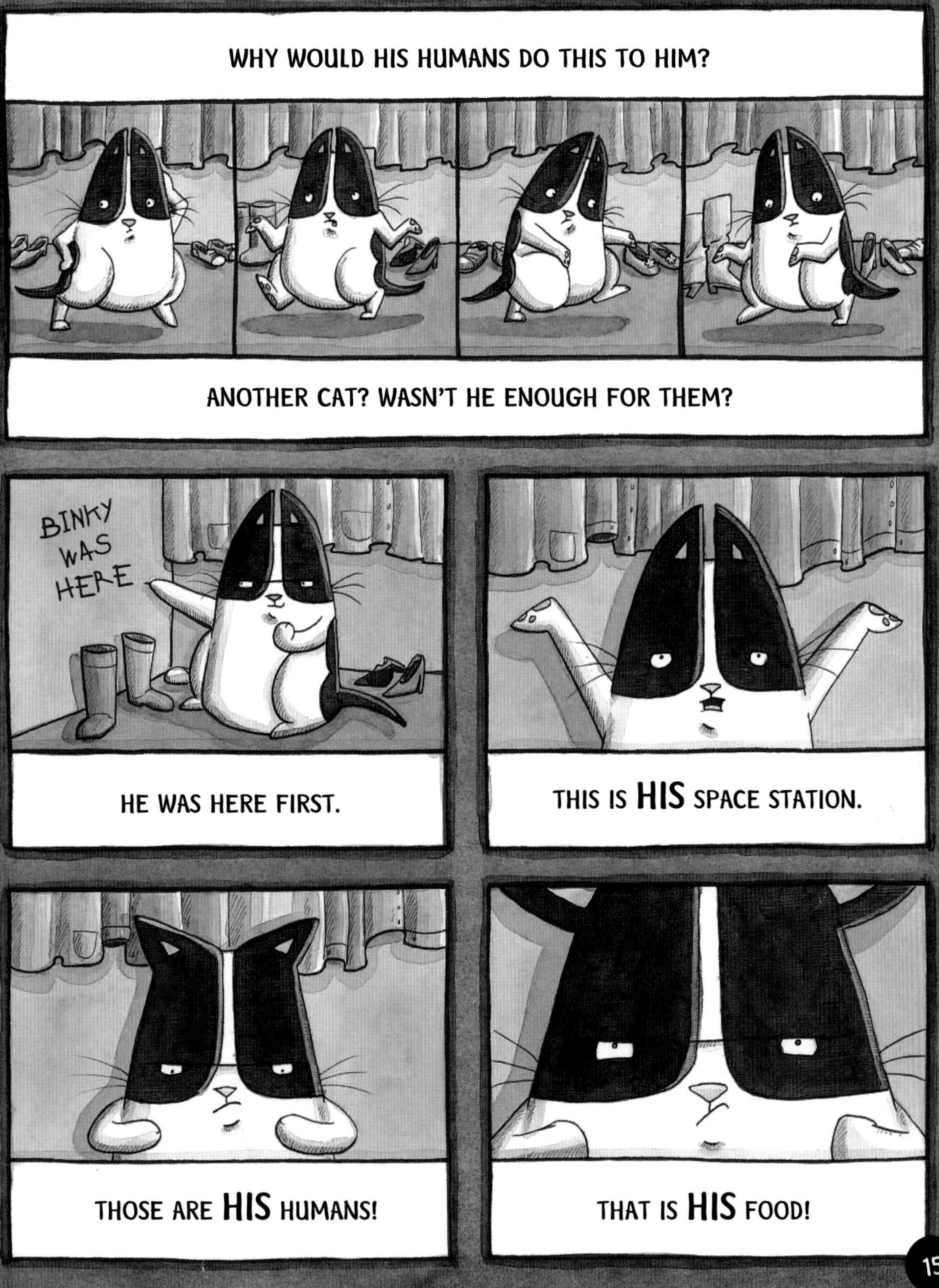
WHY WOULD HIS HUMANS DO THIS TO HIM?
ANOTHER CAT? WASN'T HE ENOUGH FOR THEM?
BINKY WAS HERE
HE WAS HERE FIRST.
THIS IS HIS SPACE STATION.
THOSE ARE HIS HUMANS!
THAT IS HIS FOOD!

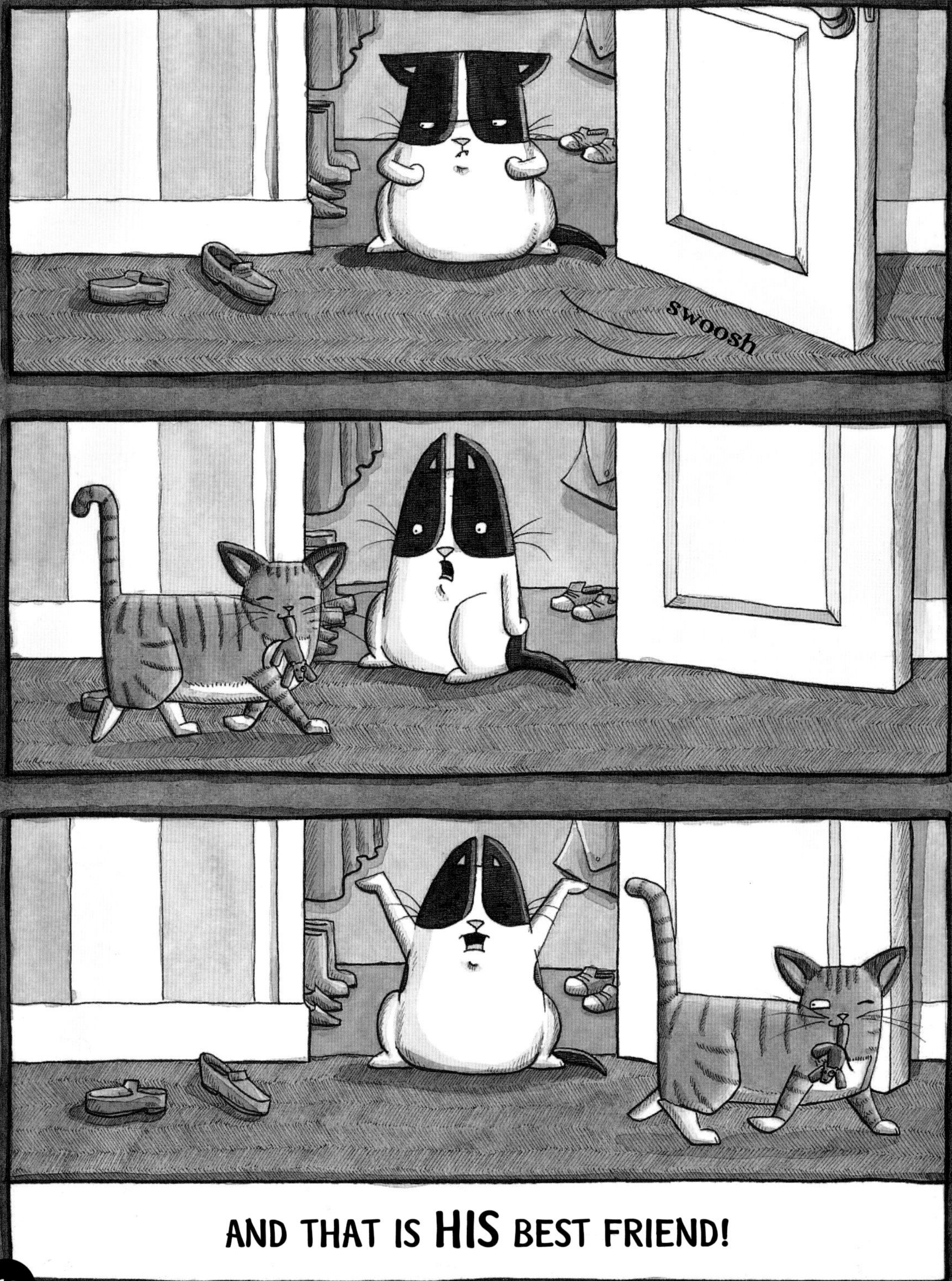
swoosh
AND THAT IS HIS BEST FRIEND!

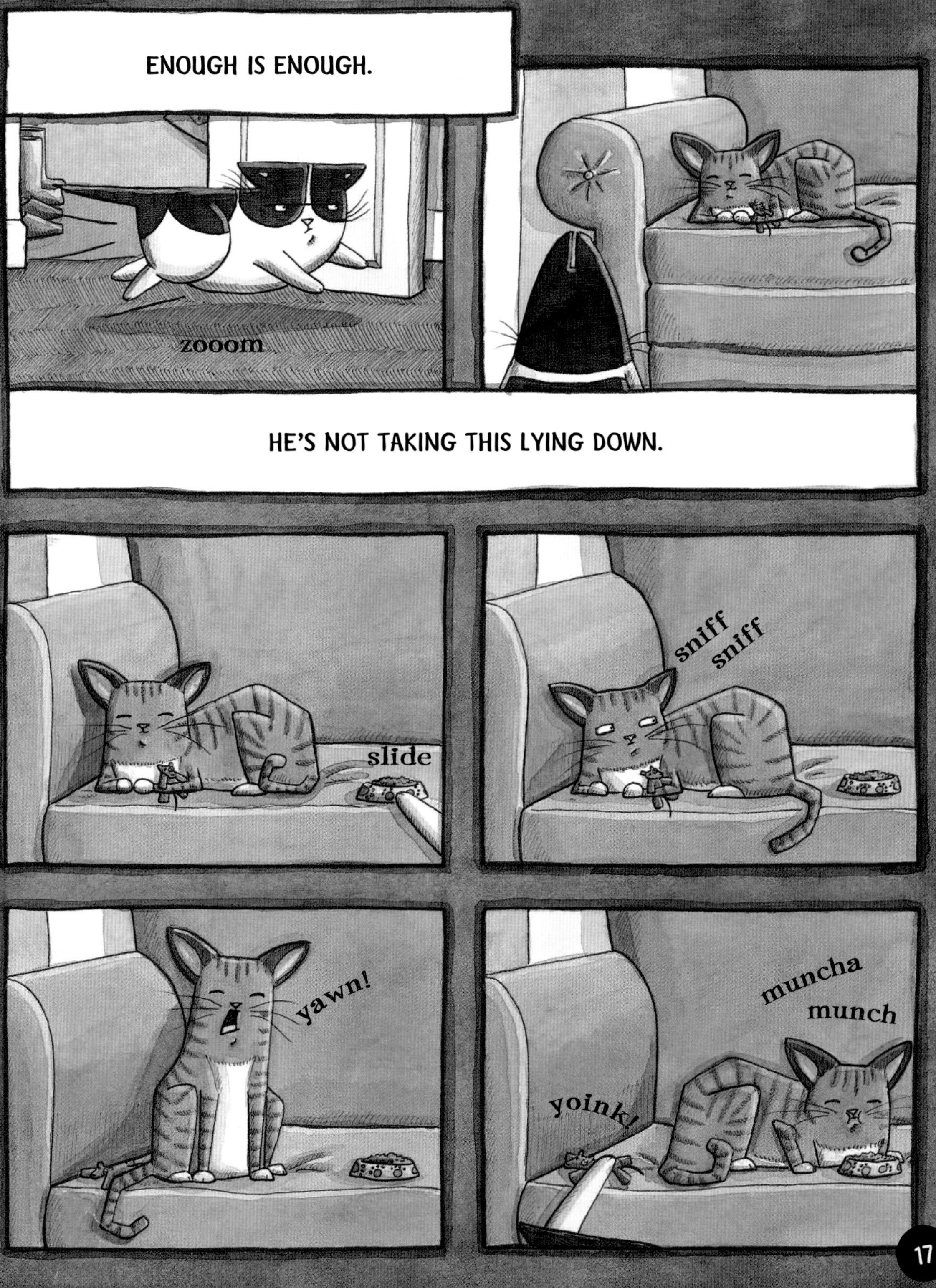

ENOUGH IS ENOUGH.
zooom
HE'S NOT TAKING THIS LYING DOWN.
slide
sniff
sniff
yawn!
muncha
munch
yoink!

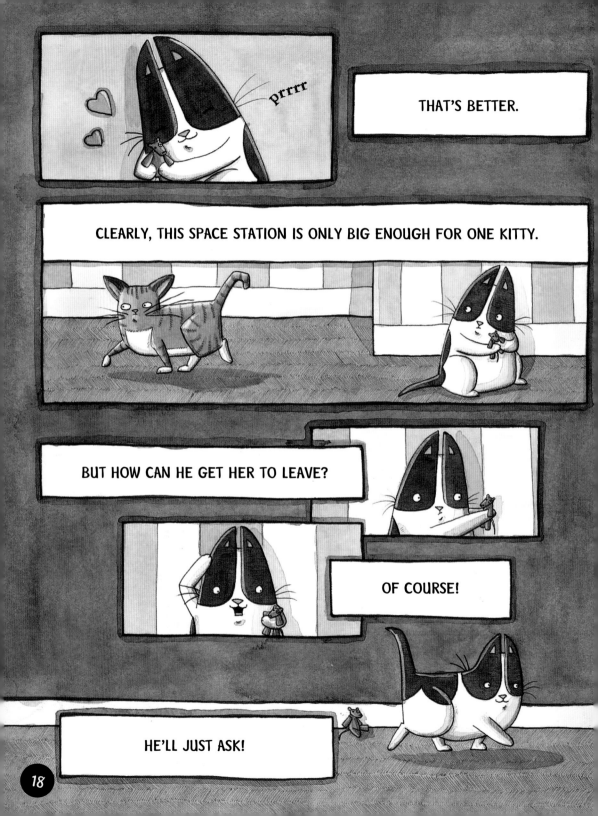

THAT'S BETTER.

CLEARLY, THIS SPACE STATION IS ONLY BIG ENOUGH FOR ONE KITTY.

BUT HOW CAN HE GET HER TO LEAVE?

OF COURSE!

HE'LL JUST ASK!

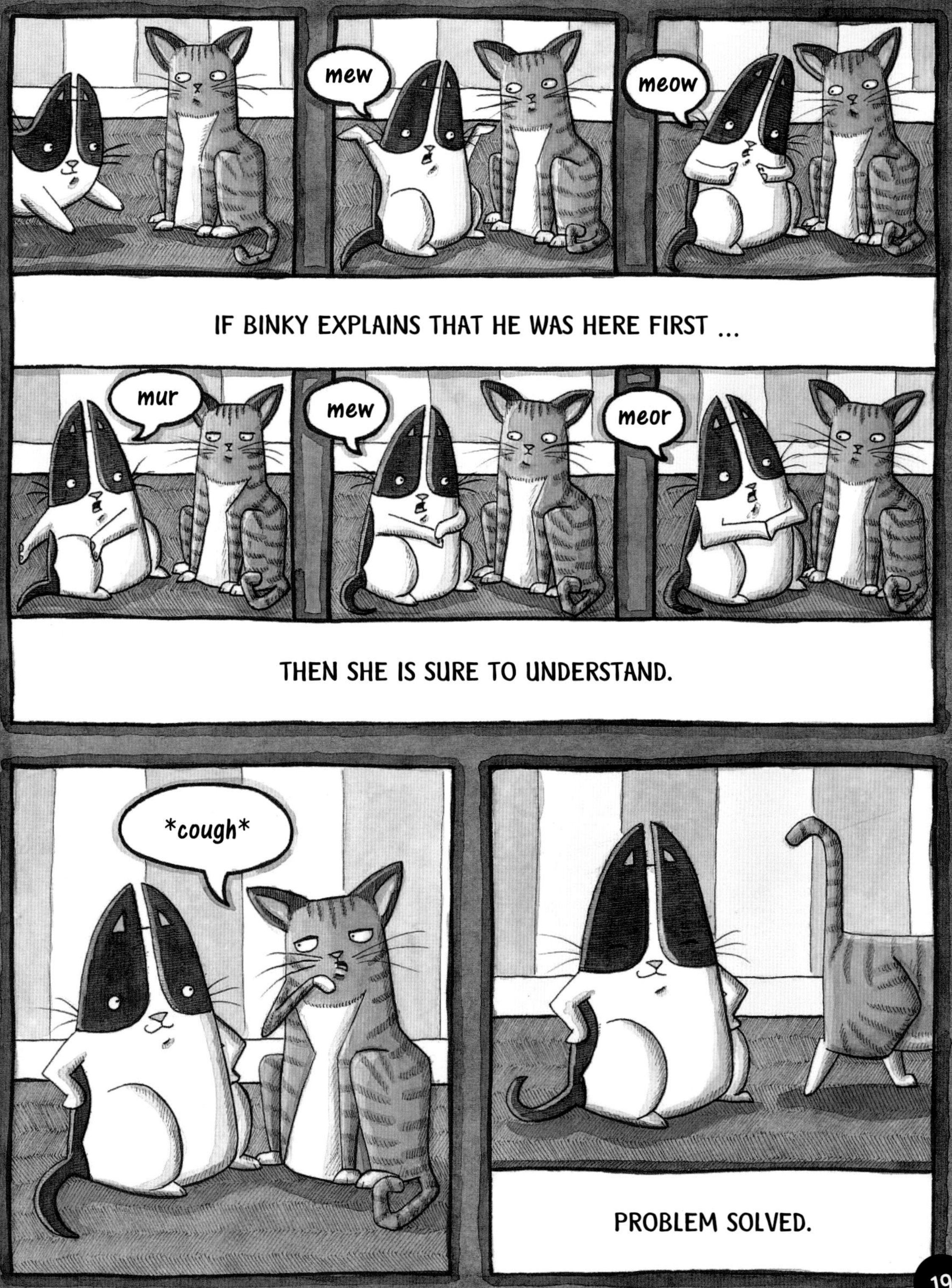
mew
meow
IF BINKY EXPLAINS THAT HE WAS HERE FIRST ...
mur
mew
meor
THEN SHE IS SURE TO UNDERSTAND.
cough
PROBLEM SOLVED.

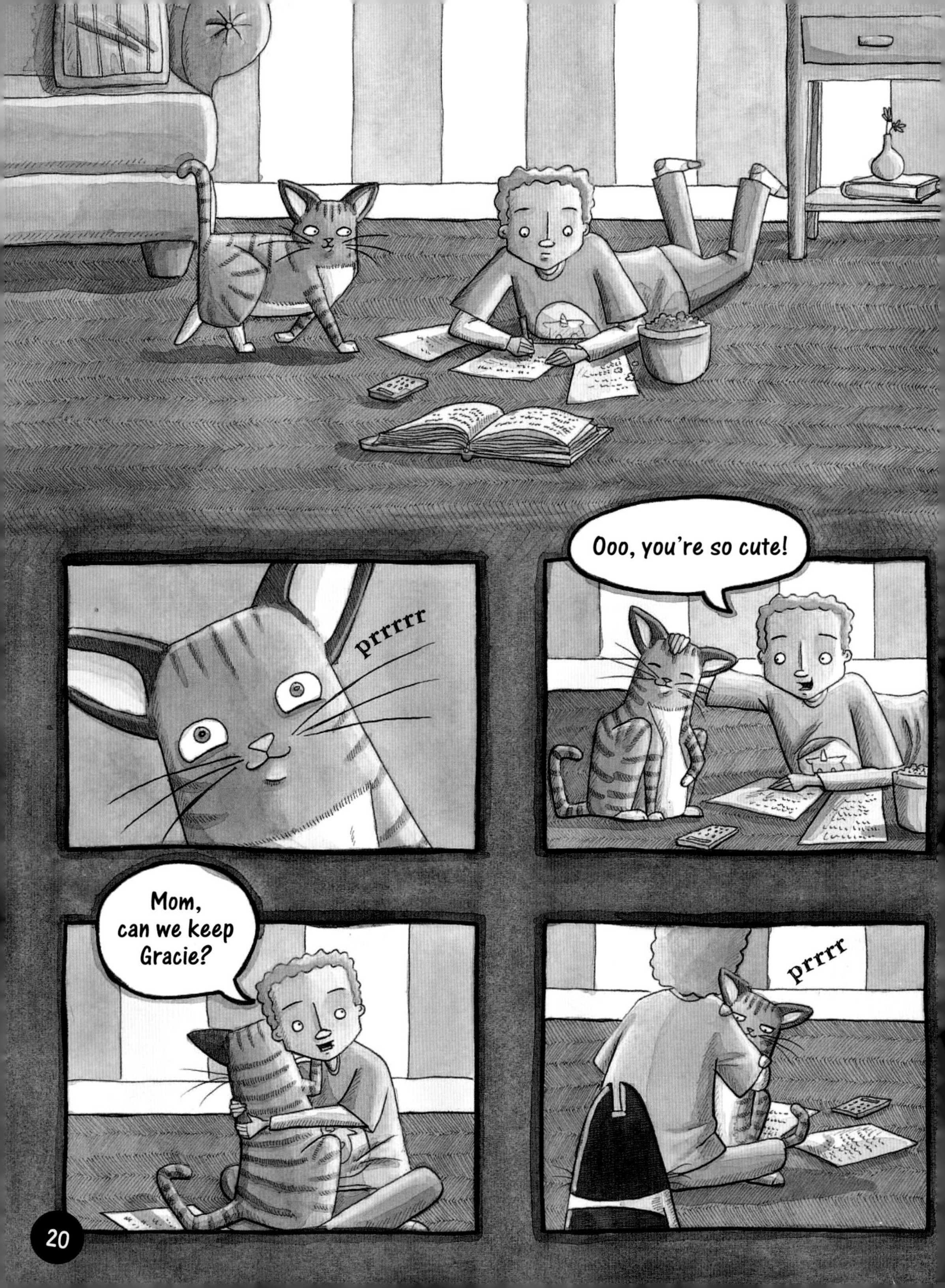
prrrrr
Ooo, you're so cute!
Mom,
can we keep
Gracie?
prrrr

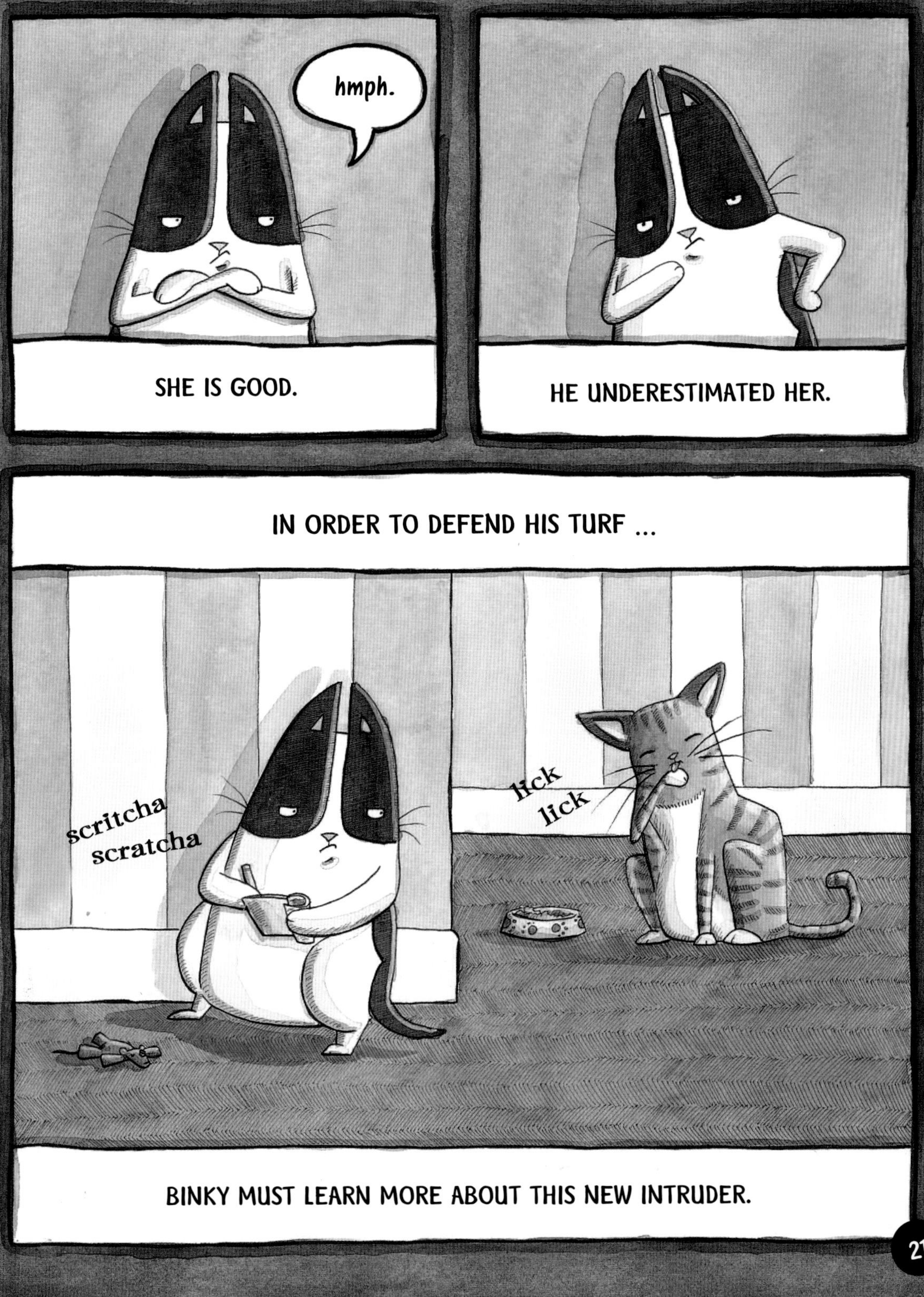
hmph.
SHE IS GOOD.
HE UNDERESTIMATED HER.
IN ORDER TO DEFEND HIS TURF ...
scritcha
scratcha
lick
lick
BINKY MUST LEARN MORE ABOUT THIS NEW INTRUDER.

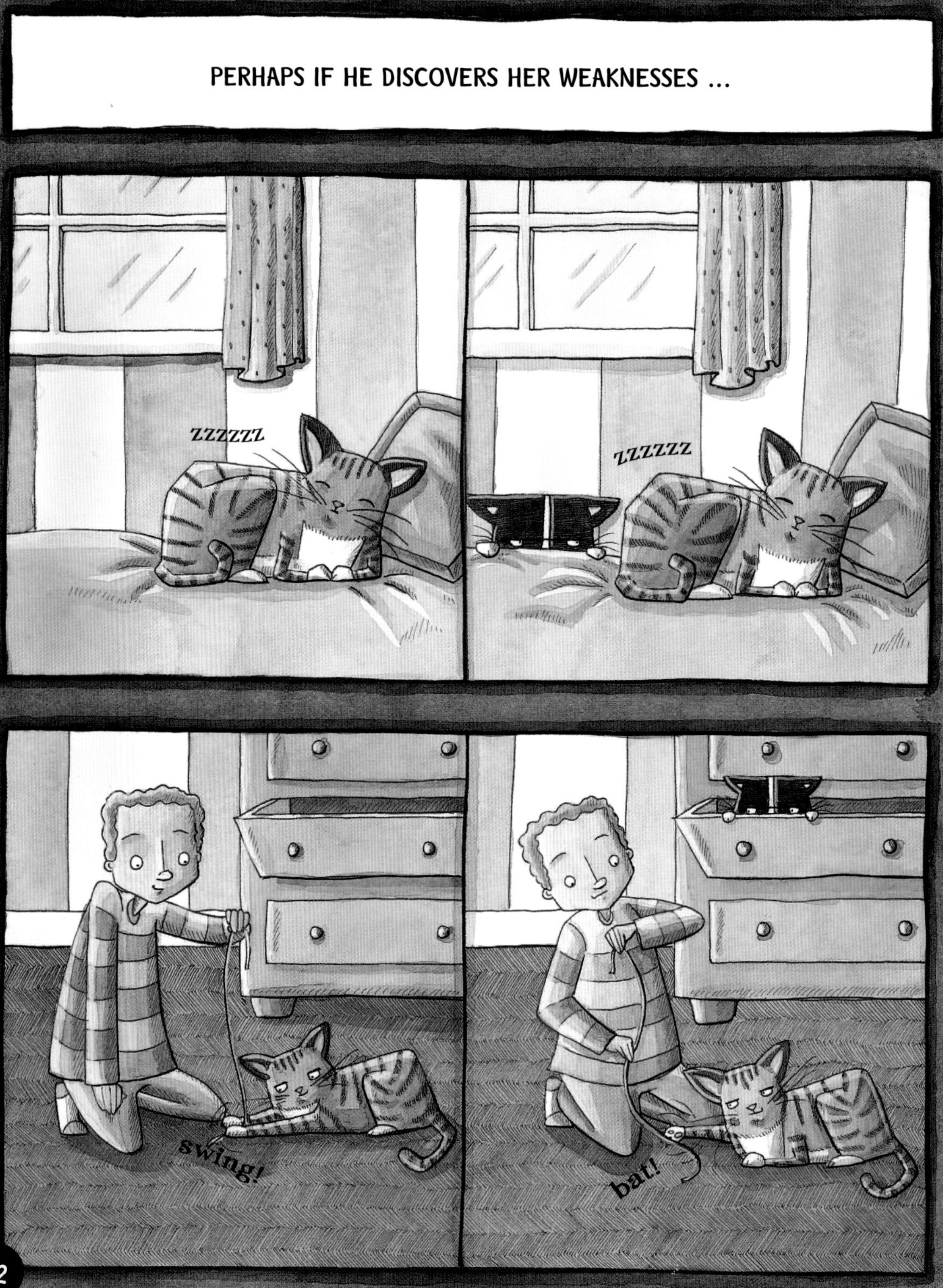
PERHAPS IF HE DISCOVERS HER WEAKNESSES ...
ZZZZZZ
ZZZZZZ
swing!
bat!

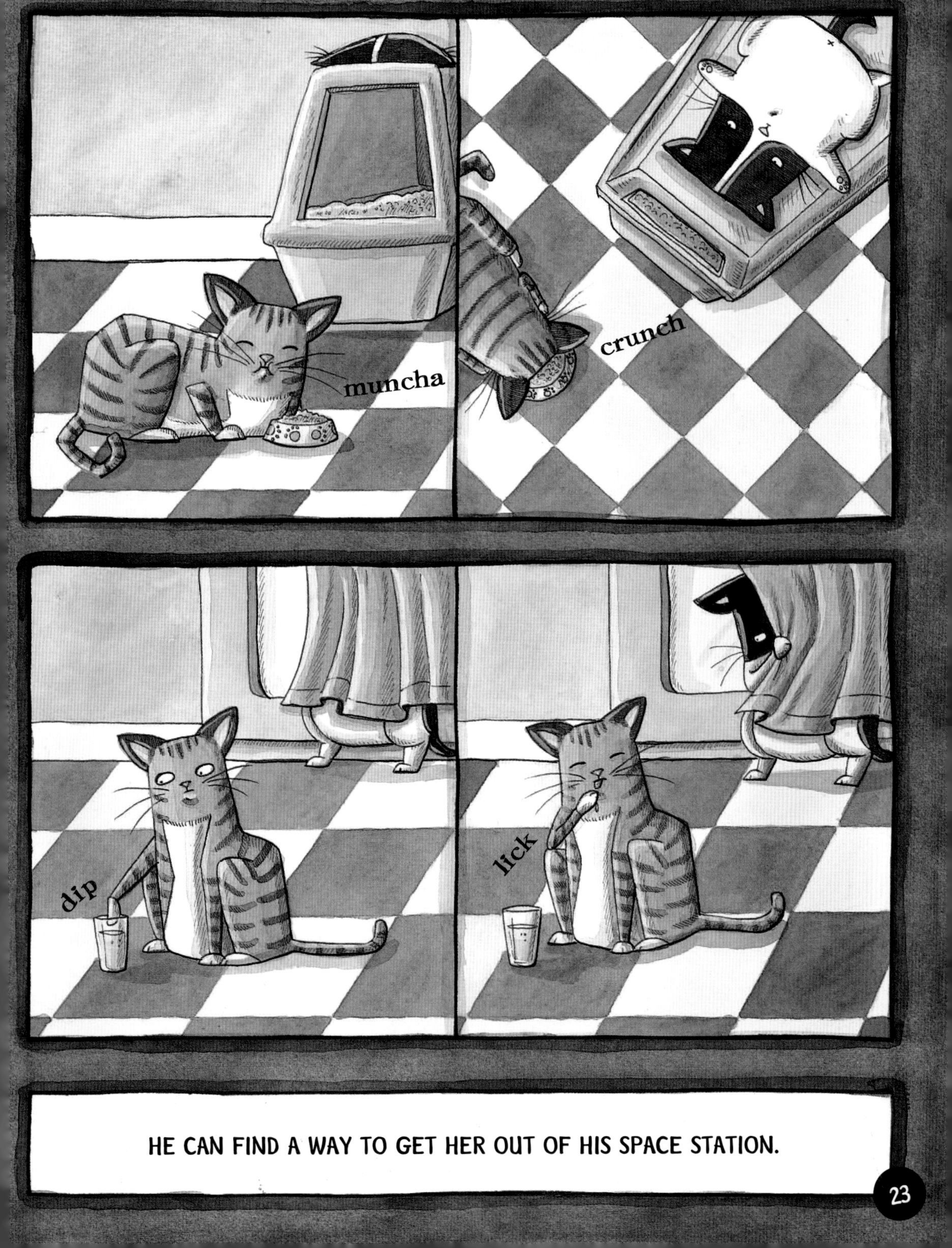
muncha
crunch
dip
lick

HE CAN FIND A WAY TO GET HER OUT OF HIS SPACE STATION.

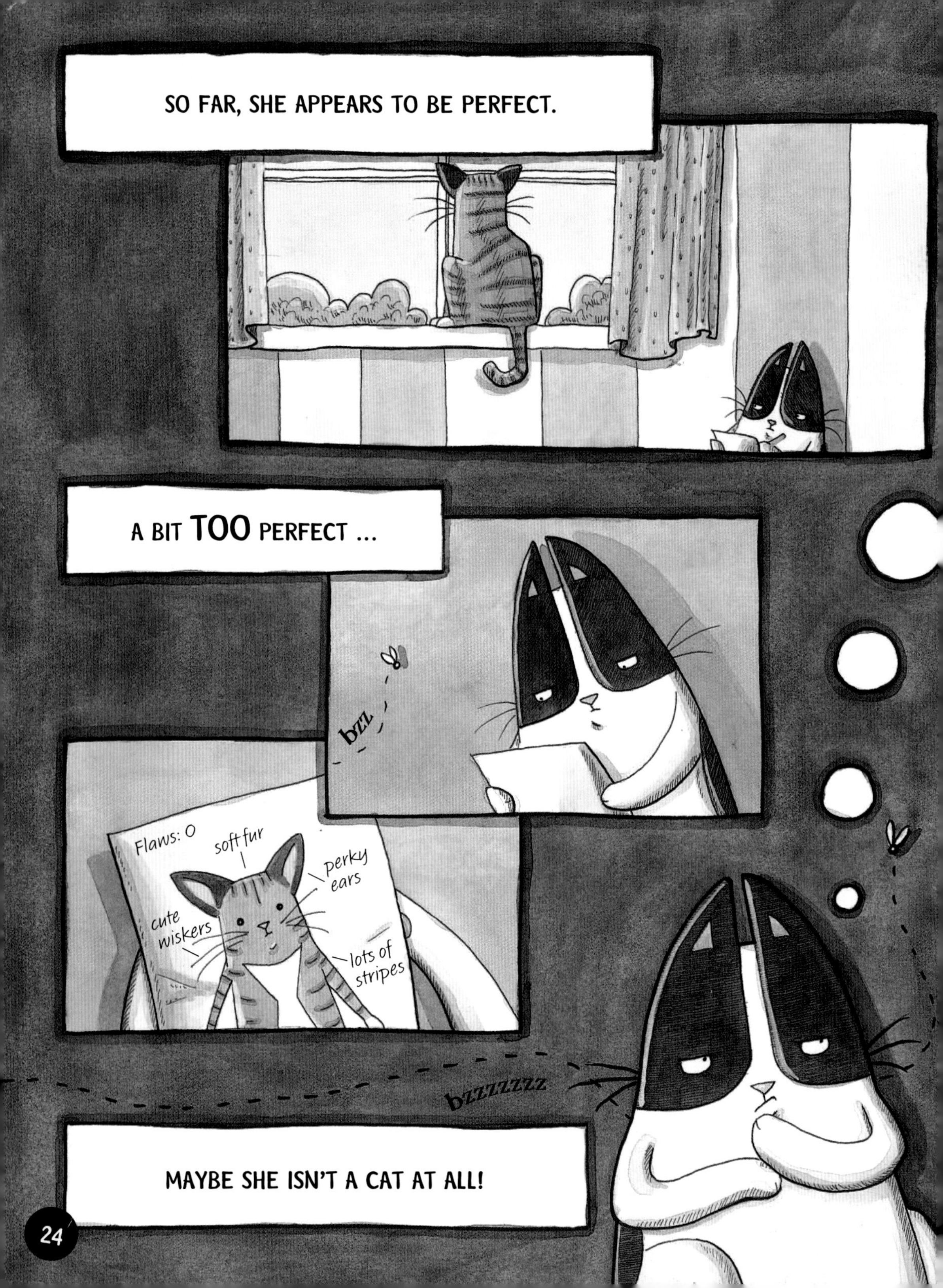
SO FAR, SHE APPEARS TO BE PERFECT.
A BIT TOO PERFECT ...
bzz
Flaws: 0
soft fur
perky ears
cute wiskers
lots of stripes
bzzzzzzz
MAYBE SHE ISN'T A CAT AT ALL!

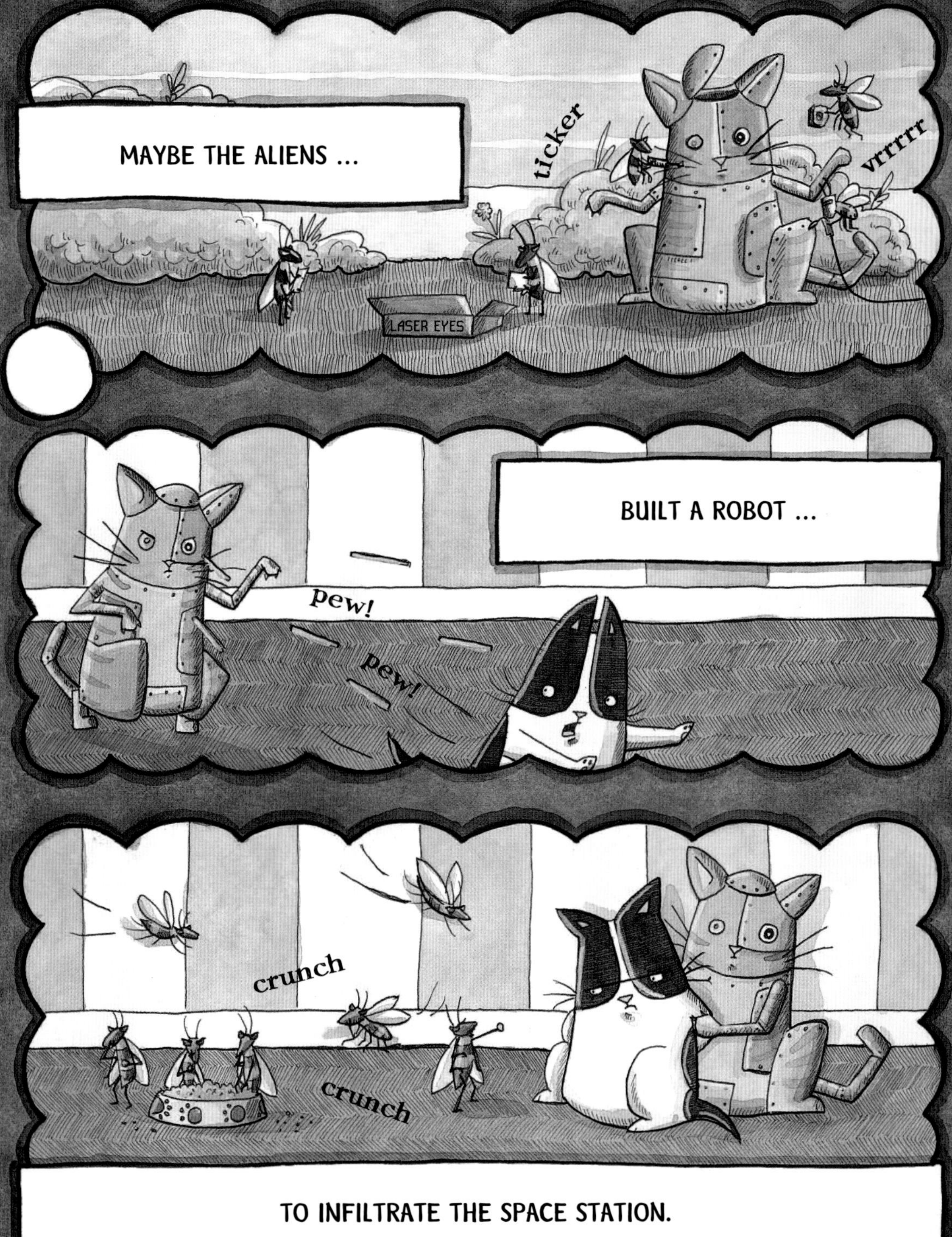
MAYBE THE ALIENS ...
ticker
vrrrrr
LASER EYES
BUILT A ROBOT ...
pew!
pew!
crunch
crunch
TO INFILTRATE THE SPACE STATION.

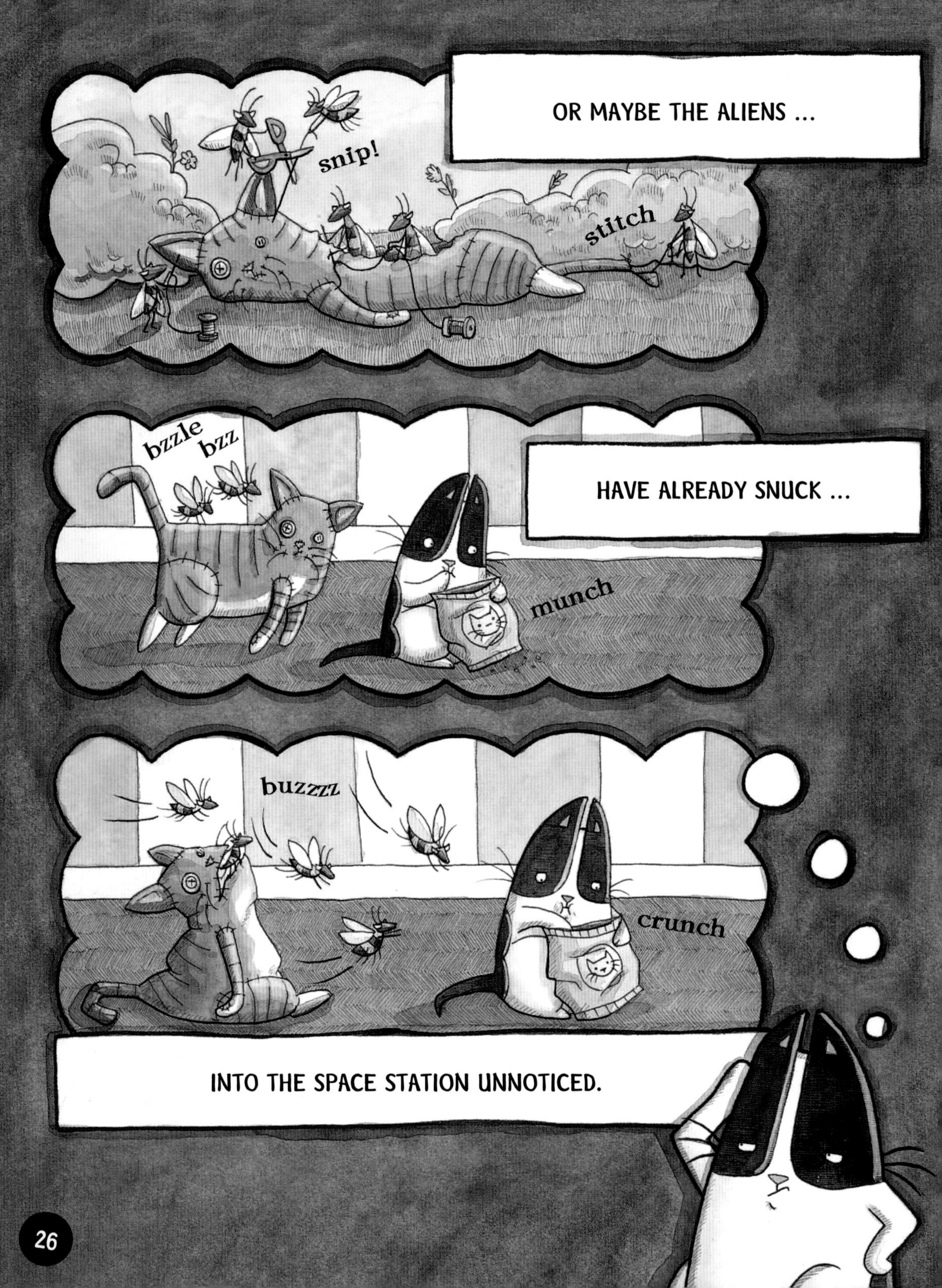

OR MAYBE THE ALIENS ...
snip!
stitch
HAVE ALREADY SNUCK ...
bzzle
bzz
munch
buzzzz
crunch
INTO THE SPACE STATION UNNOTICED.

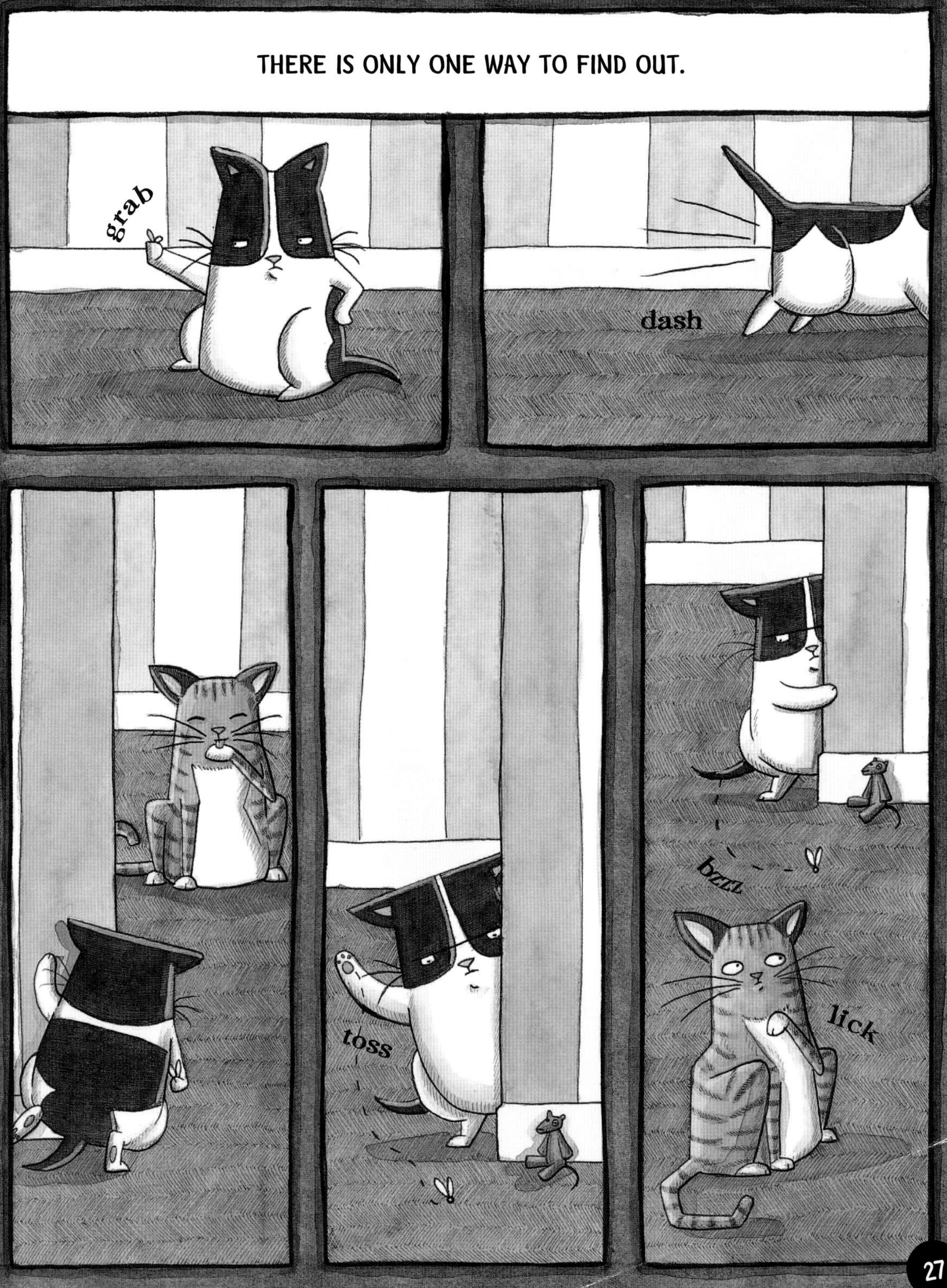
THERE IS ONLY ONE WAY TO FIND OUT.
grab
dash
toss
bzzz
lick

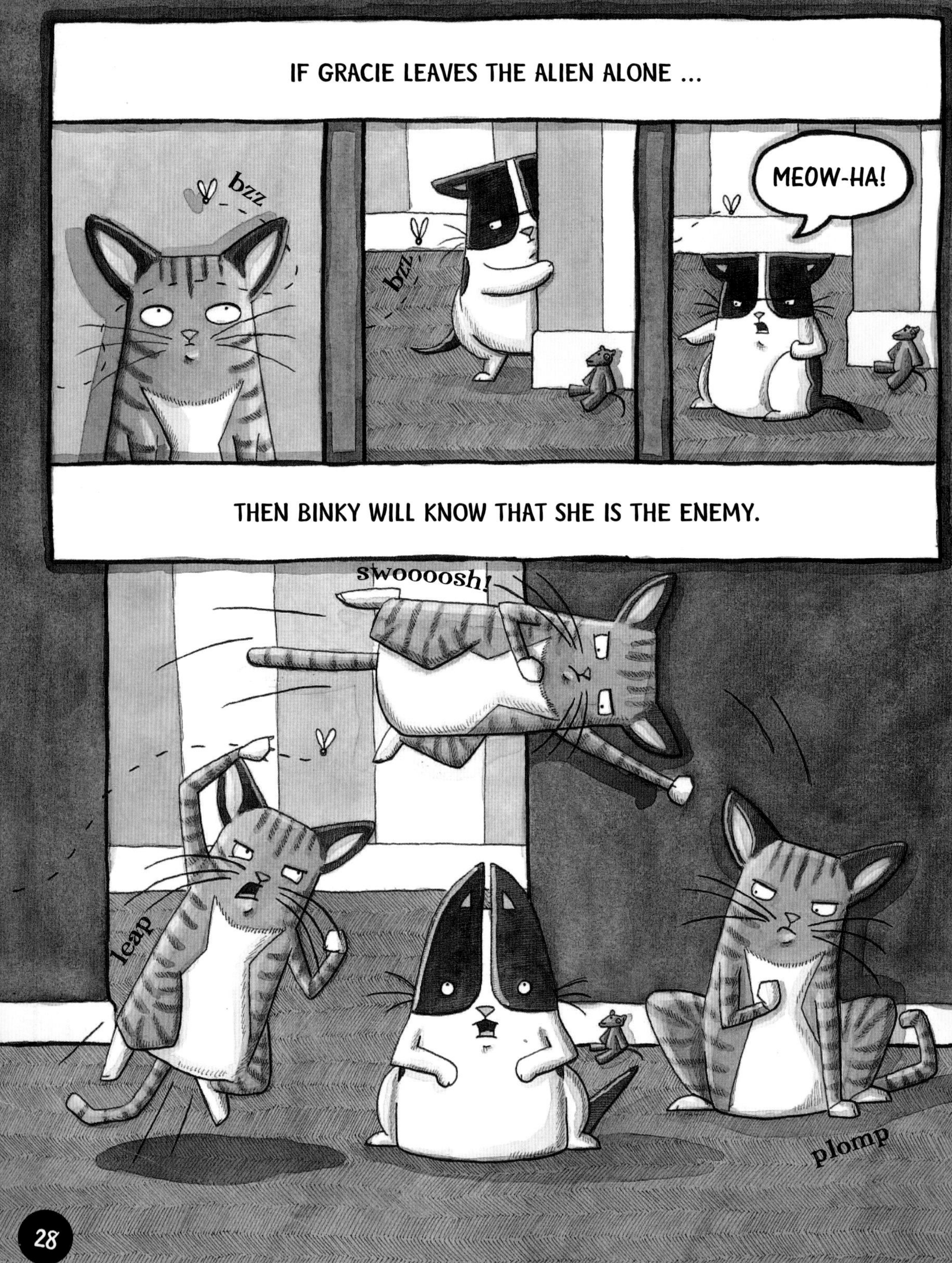
IF GRACIE LEAVES THE ALIEN ALONE ...
bzz
bzz
MEOW-HA!
THEN BINKY WILL KNOW THAT SHE IS THE ENEMY.
swooooosh!
leap
plomp

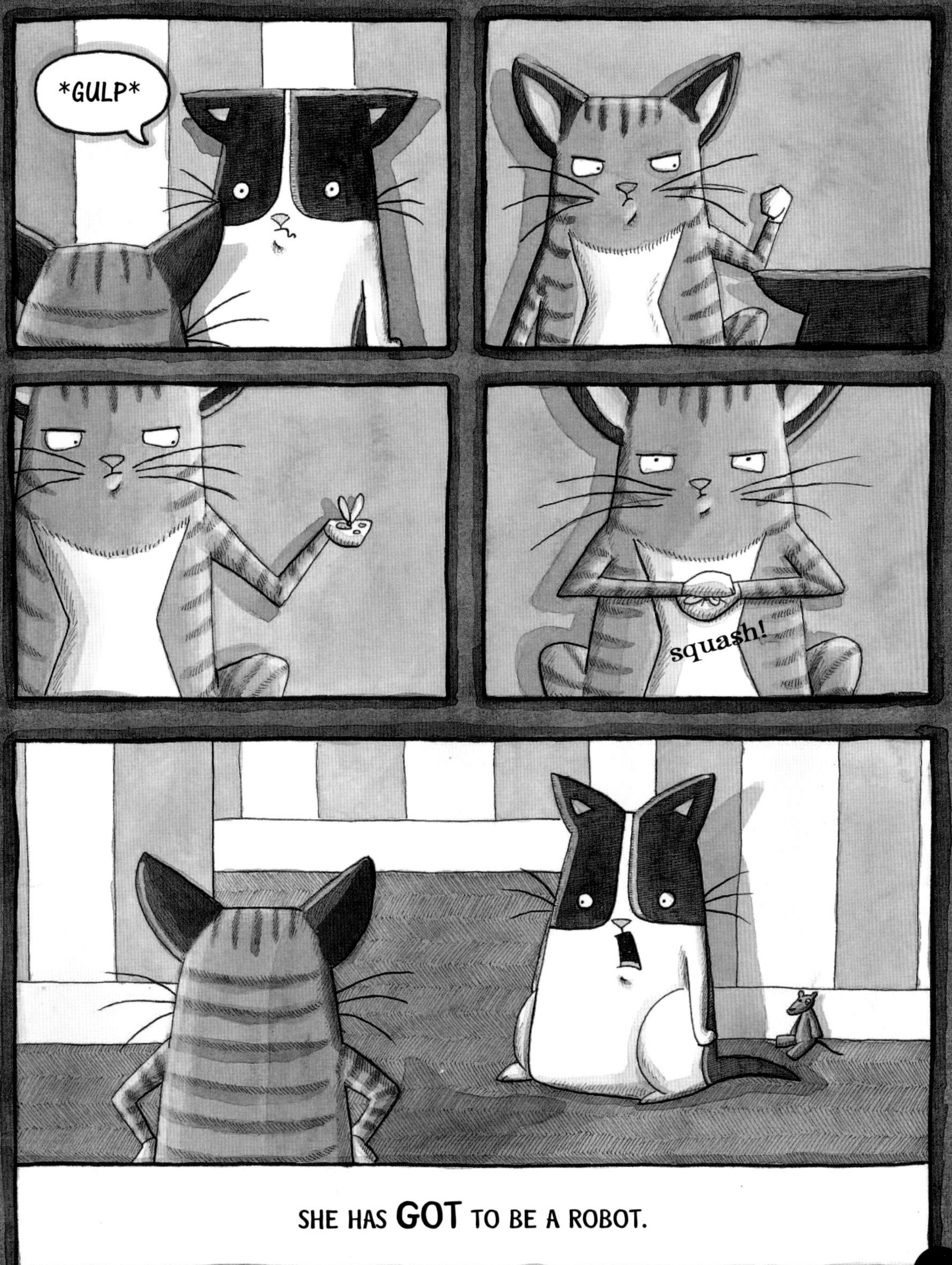
GULP
squash!
SHE HAS GOT TO BE A ROBOT.

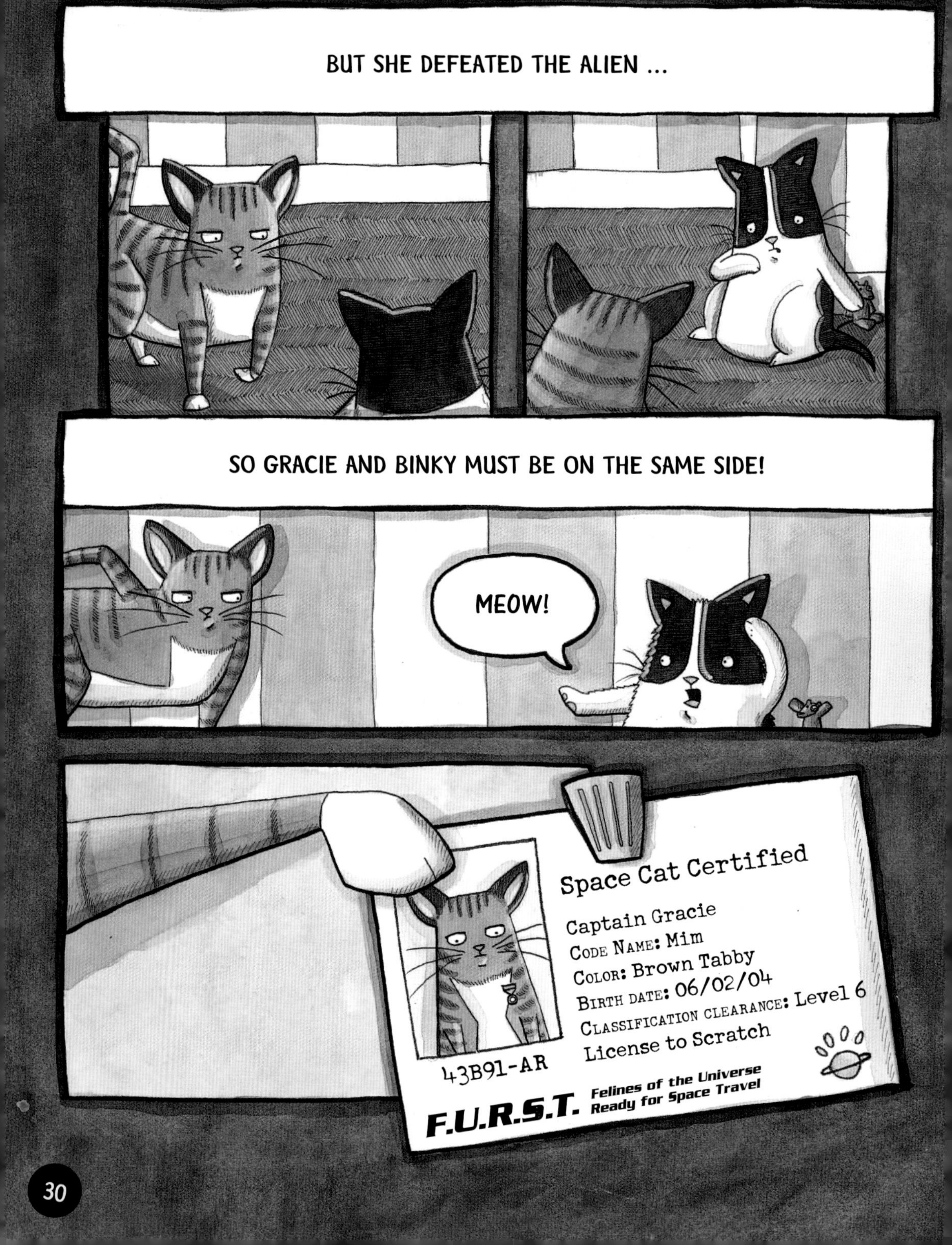
BUT SHE DEFEATED THE ALIEN ...
SO GRACIE AND BINKY MUST BE ON THE SAME SIDE!
MEOW!
Space Cat Certified
Captain Gracie
CODE NAME: Mim
COLOR: Brown Tabby
BIRTH DATE: 06/02/04
CLASSIFICATION CLEARANCE: Level 6
License to Scratch
43B91-AR
F.U.R.S.T. Felines of the Universe Ready for Space Travel

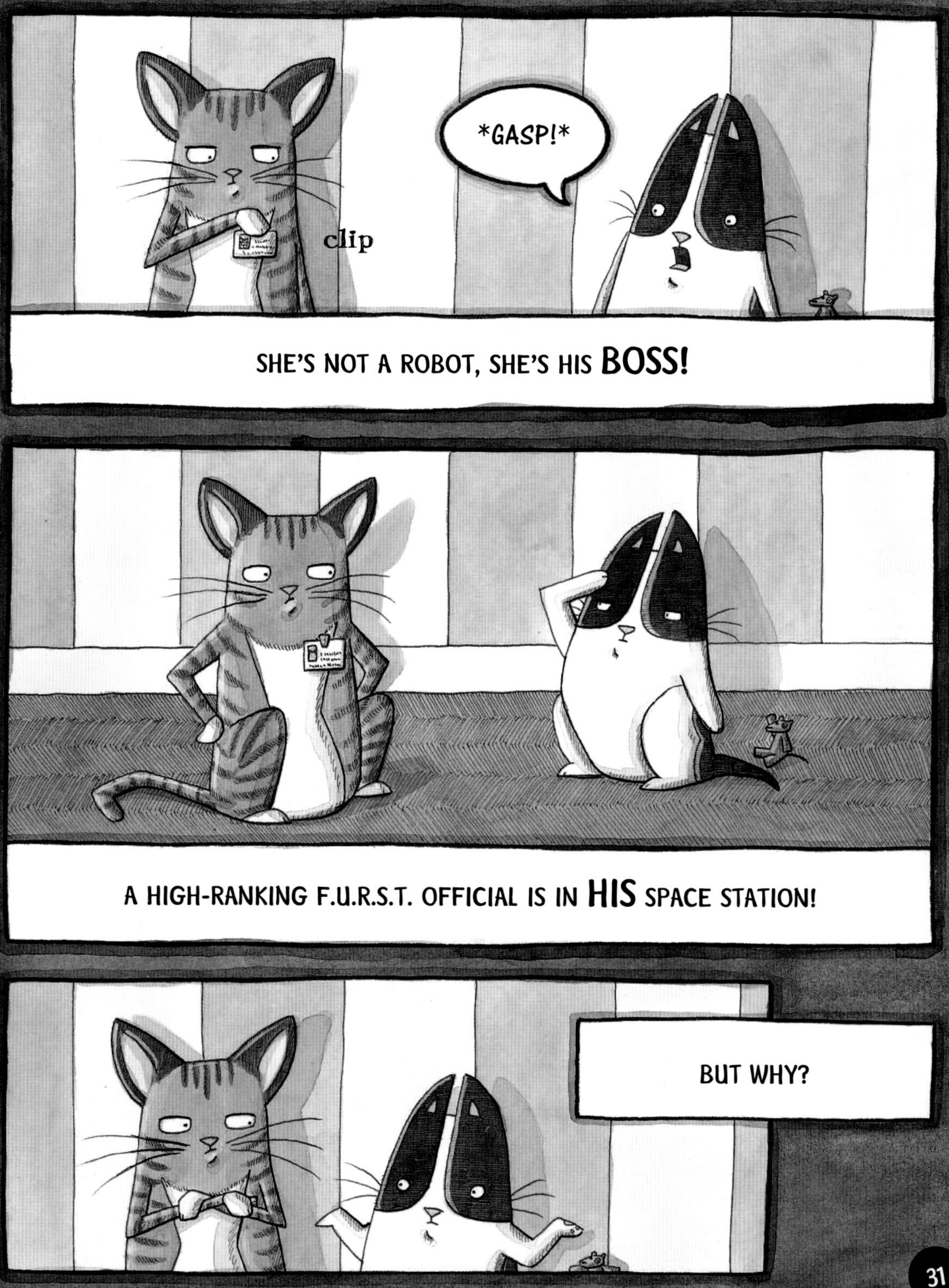

GASP!
clip
SHE'S NOT A ROBOT, SHE'S HIS BOSS!
A HIGH-RANKING F.U.R.S.T. OFFICIAL IS IN HIS SPACE STATION!
BUT WHY?

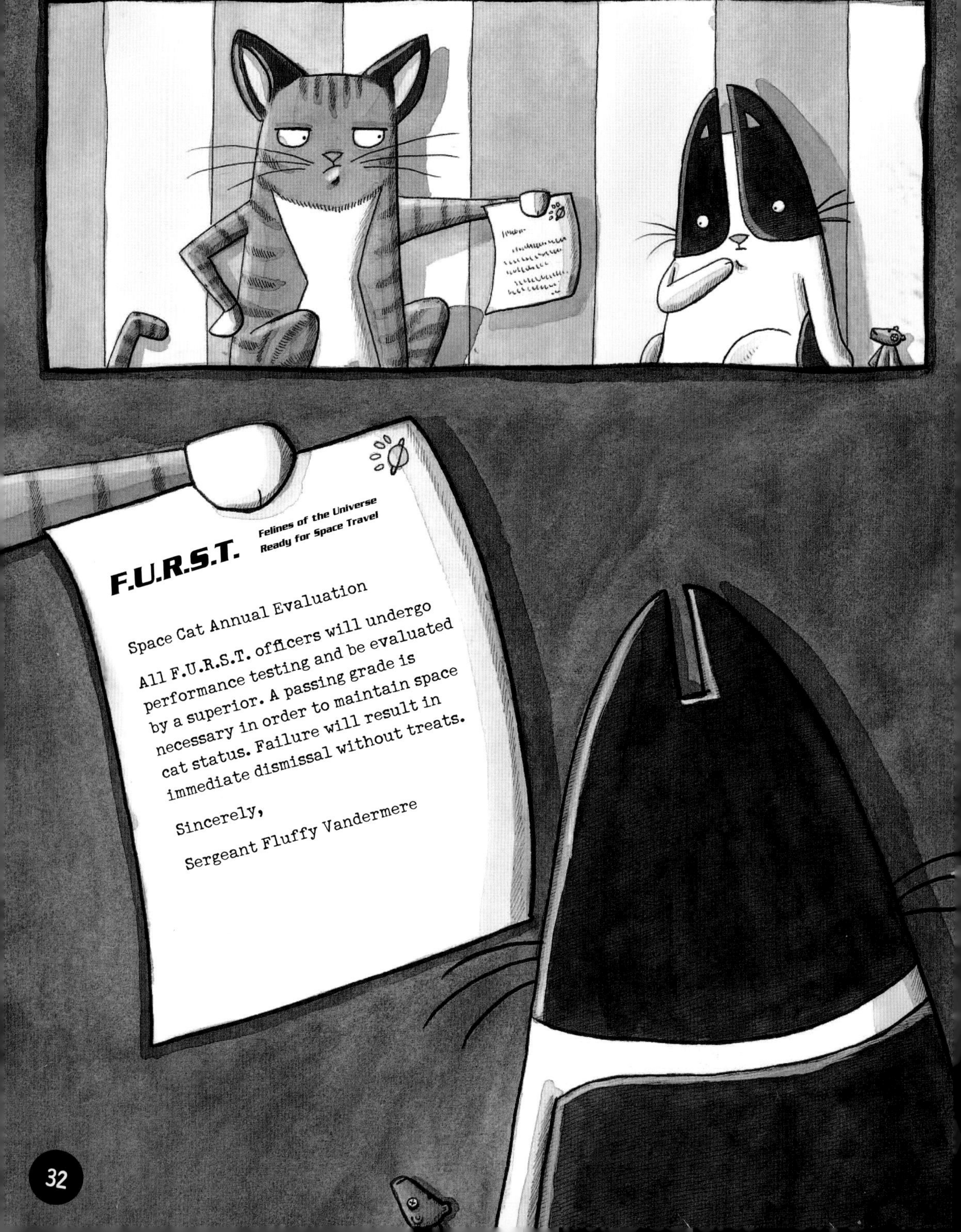

F.U.R.S.T.
Felines of the Universe Ready for Space Travel
Space Cat Annual Evaluation
All F.U.R.S.T. officers will undergo performance testing and be evaluated by a superior. A passing grade is necessary in order to maintain space cat status. Failure will result in immediate dismissal without treats.
Sincerely,
Sergeant Fluffy Vandermere

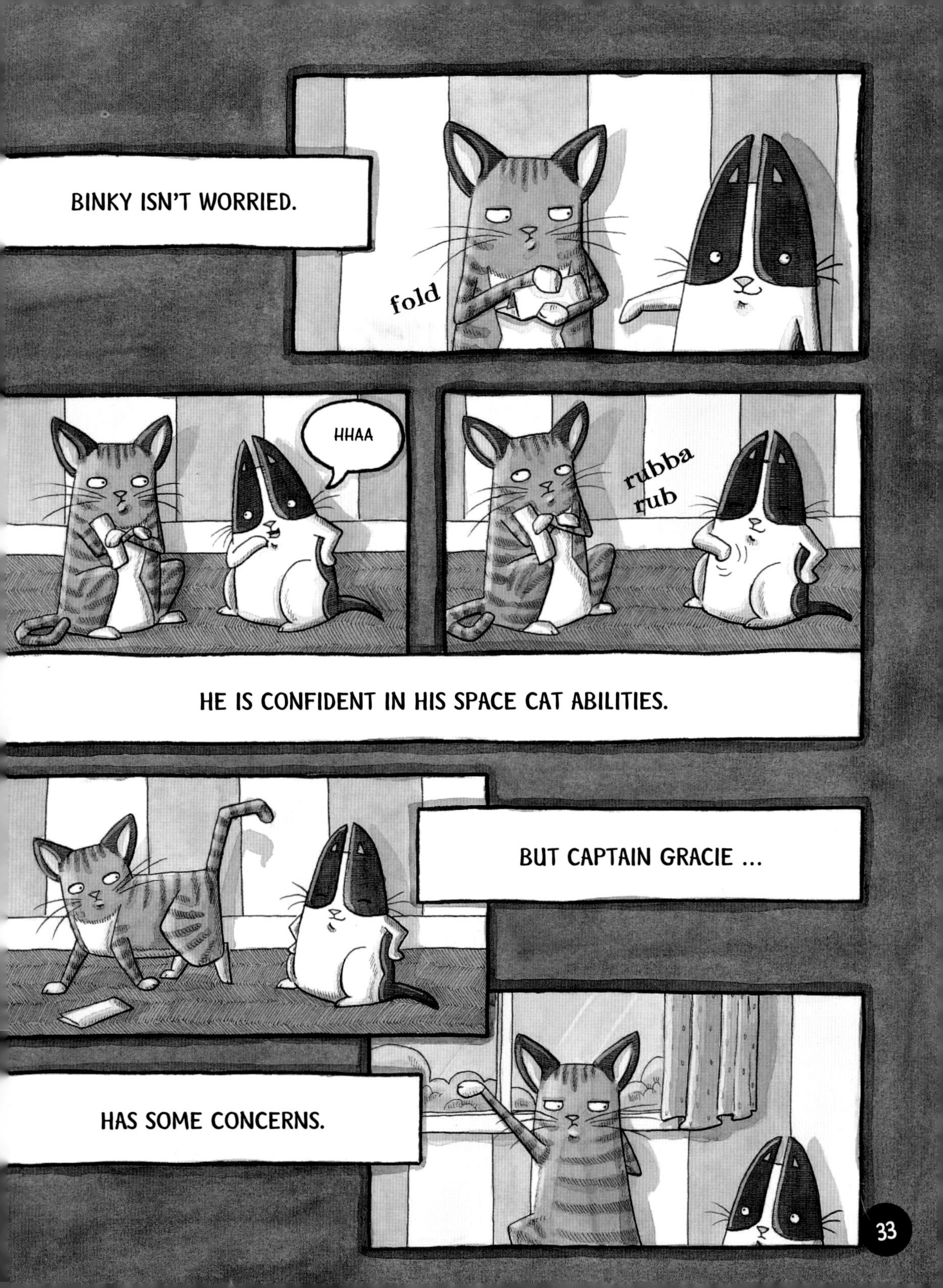
BINKY ISN'T WORRIED.
fold
HHAA
rubba rub
HE IS CONFIDENT IN HIS SPACE CAT ABILITIES.
BUT CAPTAIN GRACIE ...
HAS SOME CONCERNS.

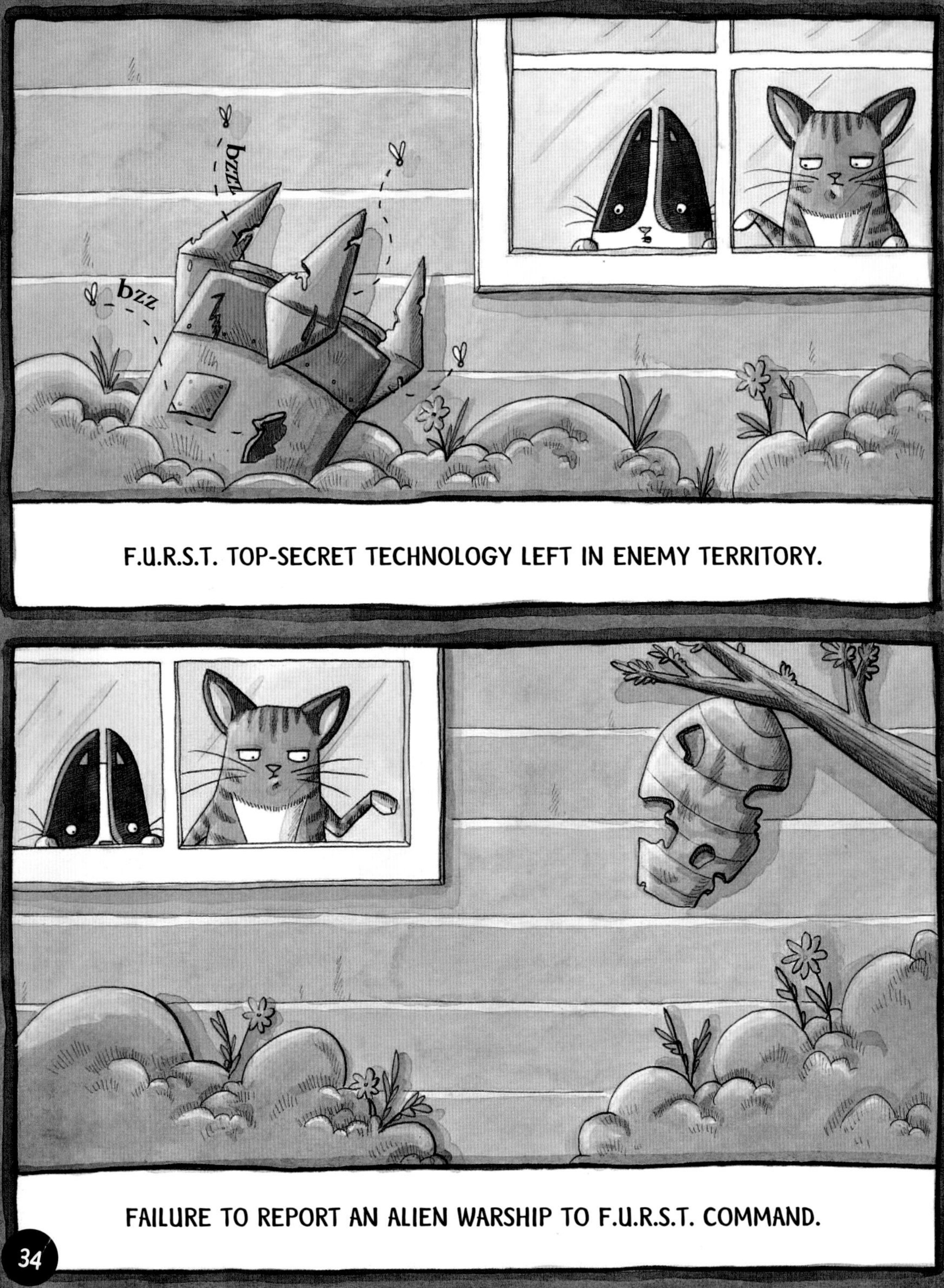
bzzz
bzz
F.U.R.S.T. TOP-SECRET TECHNOLOGY LEFT IN ENEMY TERRITORY.
FAILURE TO REPORT AN ALIEN WARSHIP TO F.U.R.S.T. COMMAND.

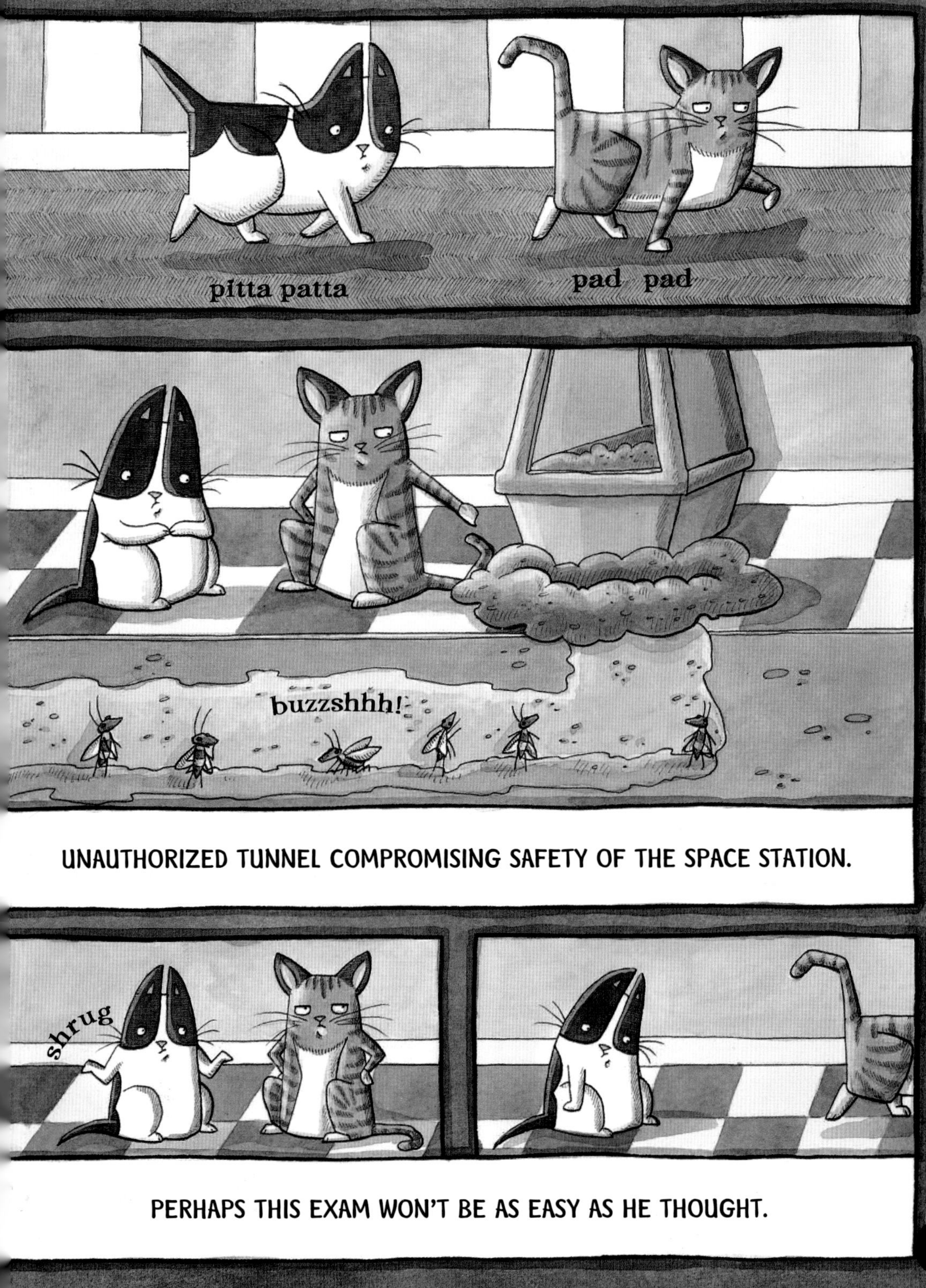
pitta patta
pad pad
buzzshhh!
UNAUTHORIZED TUNNEL COMPROMISING SAFETY OF THE SPACE STATION.
shrug
PERHAPS THIS EXAM WON'T BE AS EASY AS HE THOUGHT.

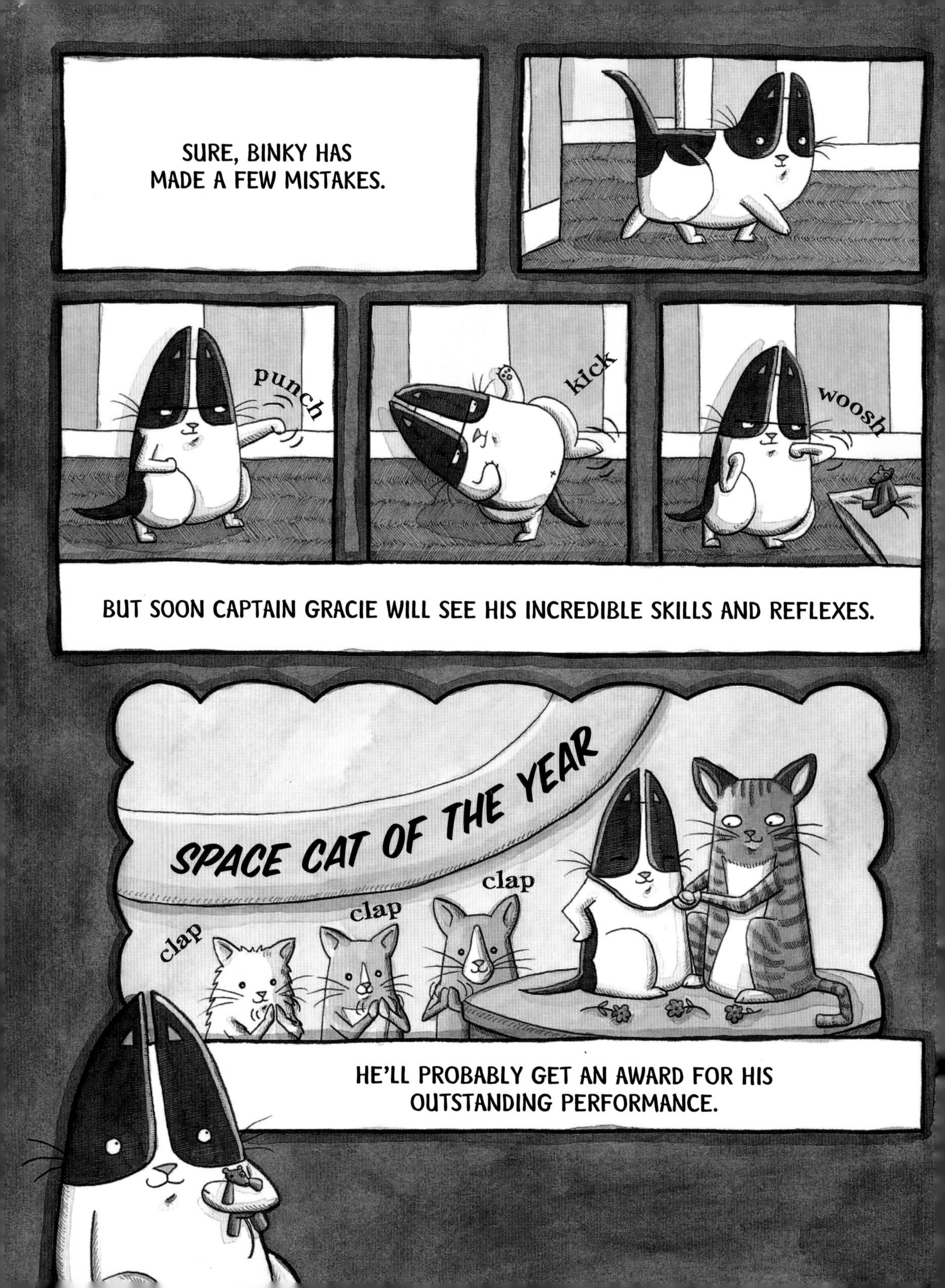
SURE, BINKY HAS MADE A FEW MISTAKES.
punch
kick
woosh
BUT SOON CAPTAIN GRACIE WILL SEE HIS INCREDIBLE SKILLS AND REFLEXES.
SPACE CAT OF THE YEAR
clap
clap
clap
HE'LL PROBABLY GET AN AWARD FOR HIS OUTSTANDING PERFORMANCE.

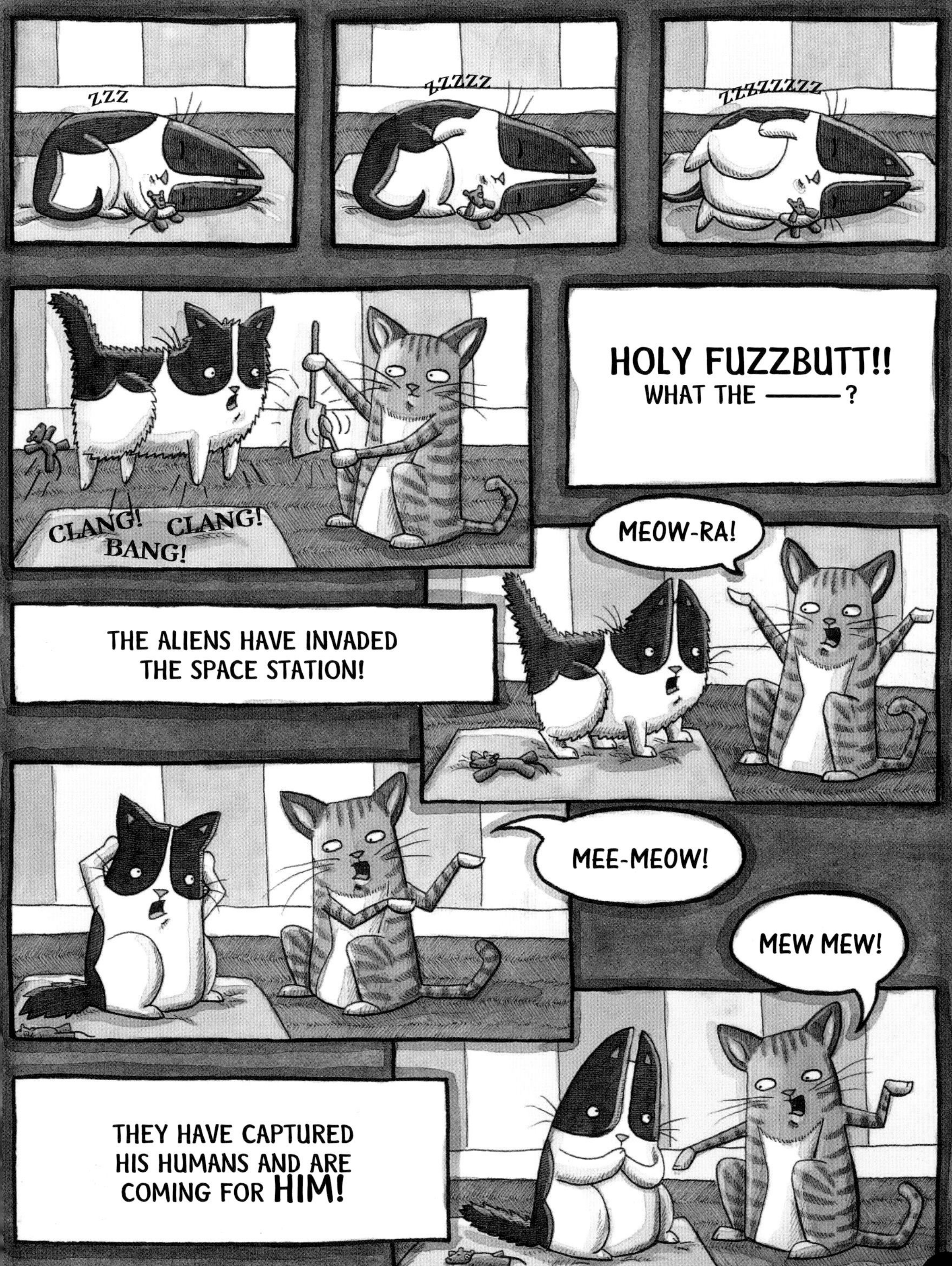

ZZZ
ZZZZZ
ZZZZZZZZ
CLANG! CLANG!
BANG!
HOLY FUZZBUTT!!
WHAT THE ——?
MEOW-RA!
THE ALIENS HAVE INVADED THE SPACE STATION!
MEE-MEOW!
MEW MEW!
THEY HAVE CAPTURED HIS HUMANS AND ARE COMING FOR HIM!

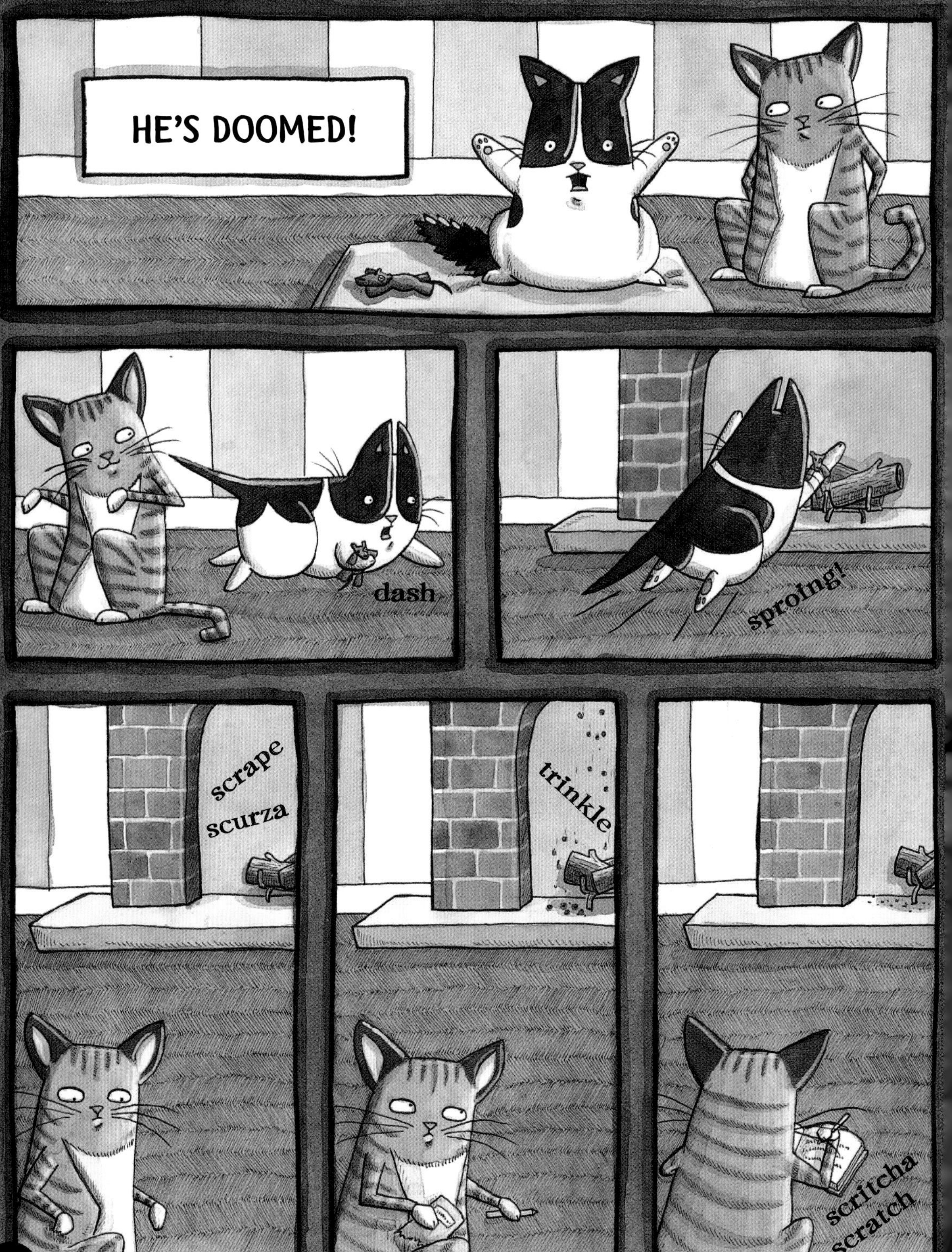
HE'S DOOMED!
dash
sproing!
scrape
scurza
trinkle
scritcha
scratch

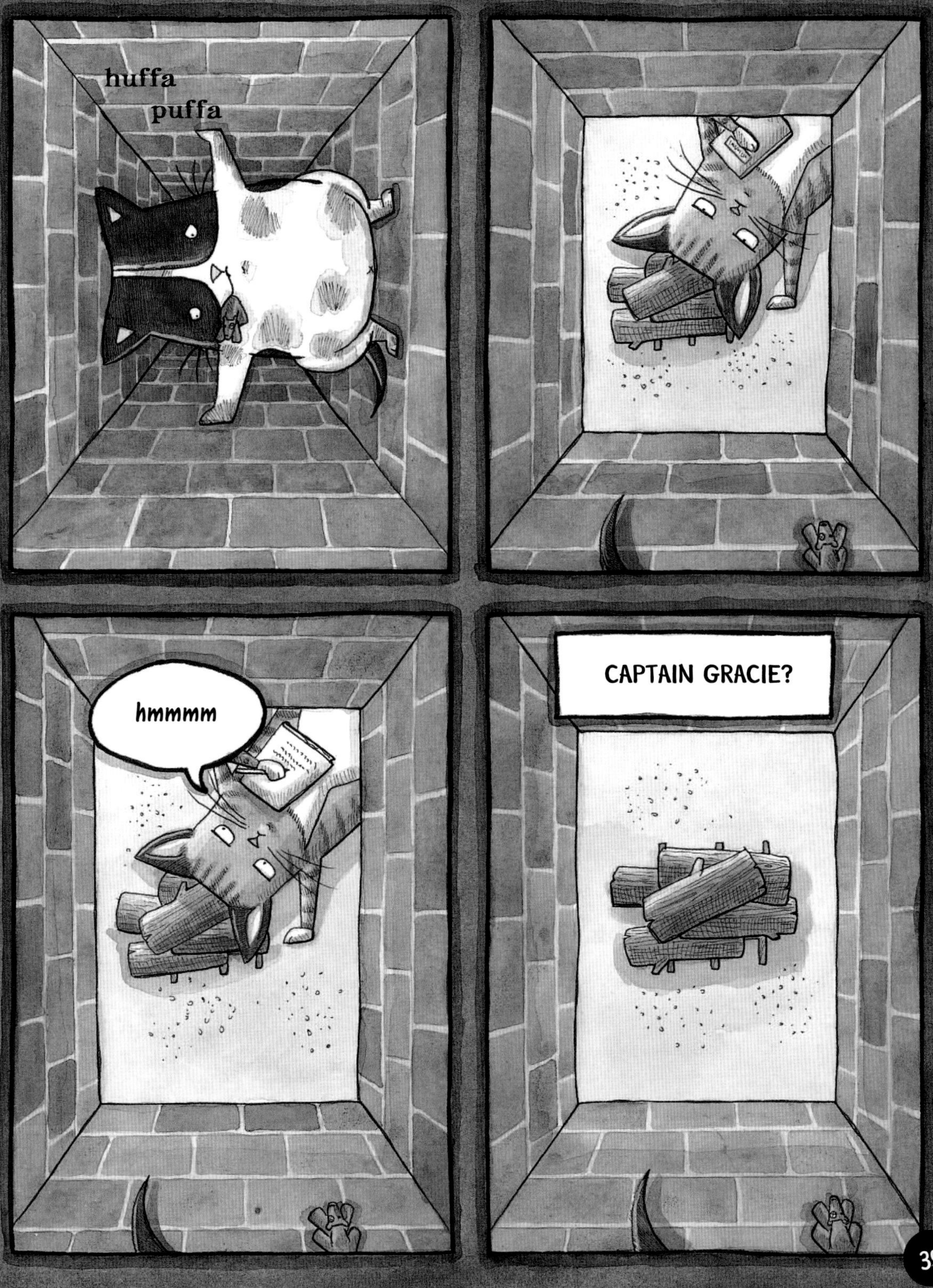
huffa
puffa
hmmmm
CAPTAIN GRACIE?

wibble *wobble*

WHERE IS CAPTAIN GRACIE? DID THE ALIENS GET HER?

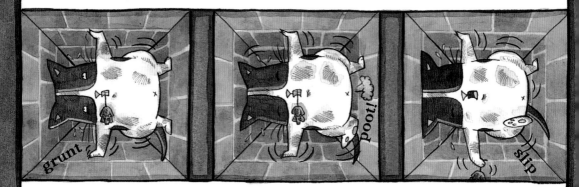

grunt *poot!* *slip*

BINKY MUST STAY HIDDEN, BUT HE CAN'T HOLD ON MUCH LONGER ...

BOOOM!

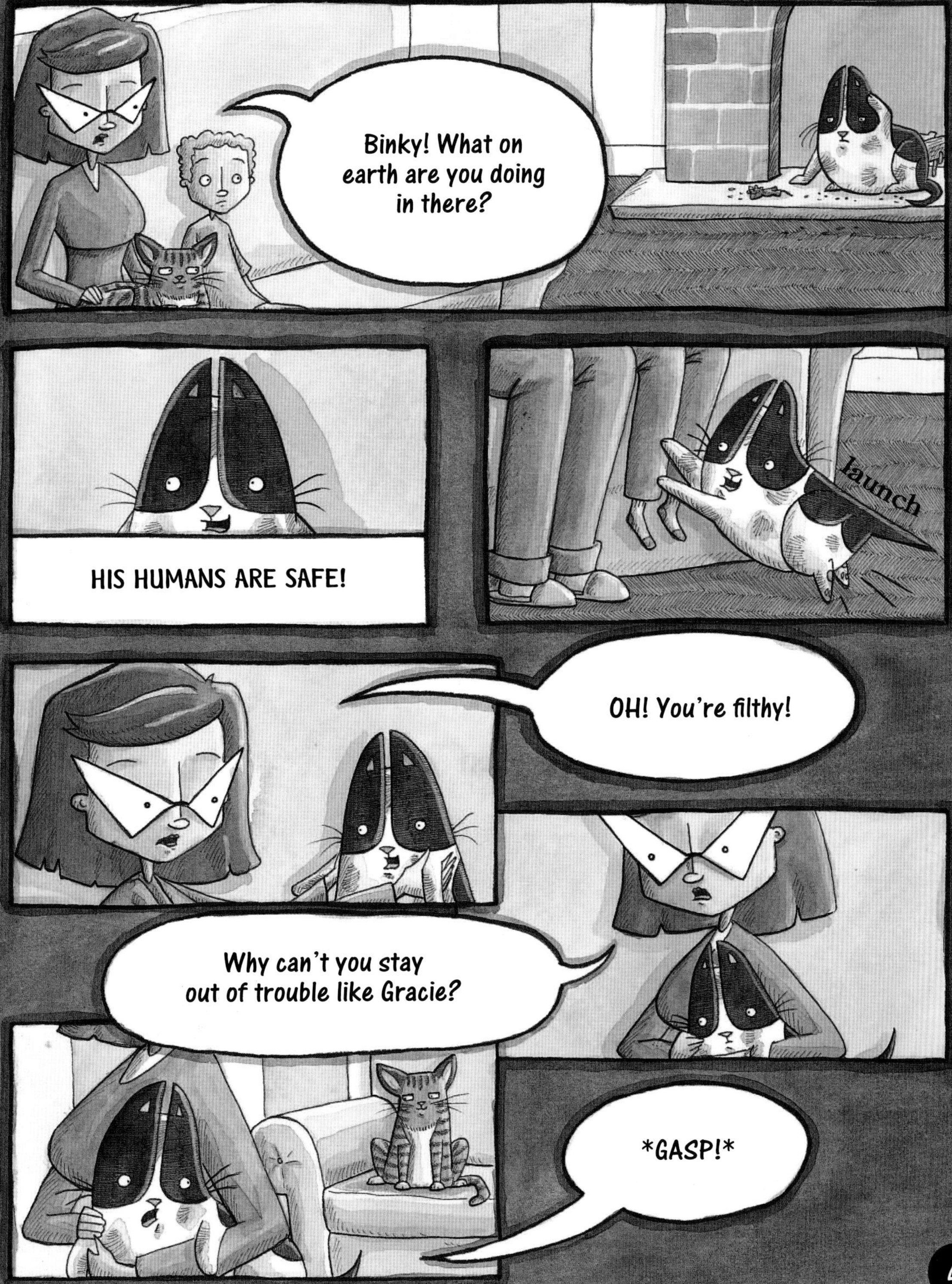
Binky! What on earth are you doing in there?
HIS HUMANS ARE SAFE!
launch
OH! You're filthy!
Why can't you stay out of trouble like Gracie?
GASP!

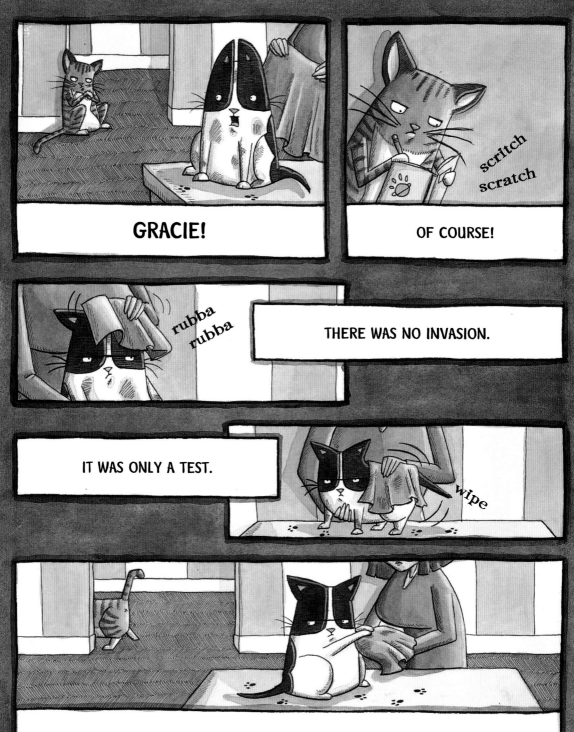

GRACIE!

OF COURSE!

scritch scratch

rubba rubba

THERE WAS NO INVASION.

IT WAS ONLY A TEST.

wipe

IF THIS IS WHAT GIRLS ARE LIKE, HE'S GLAD HE'S FIXED.

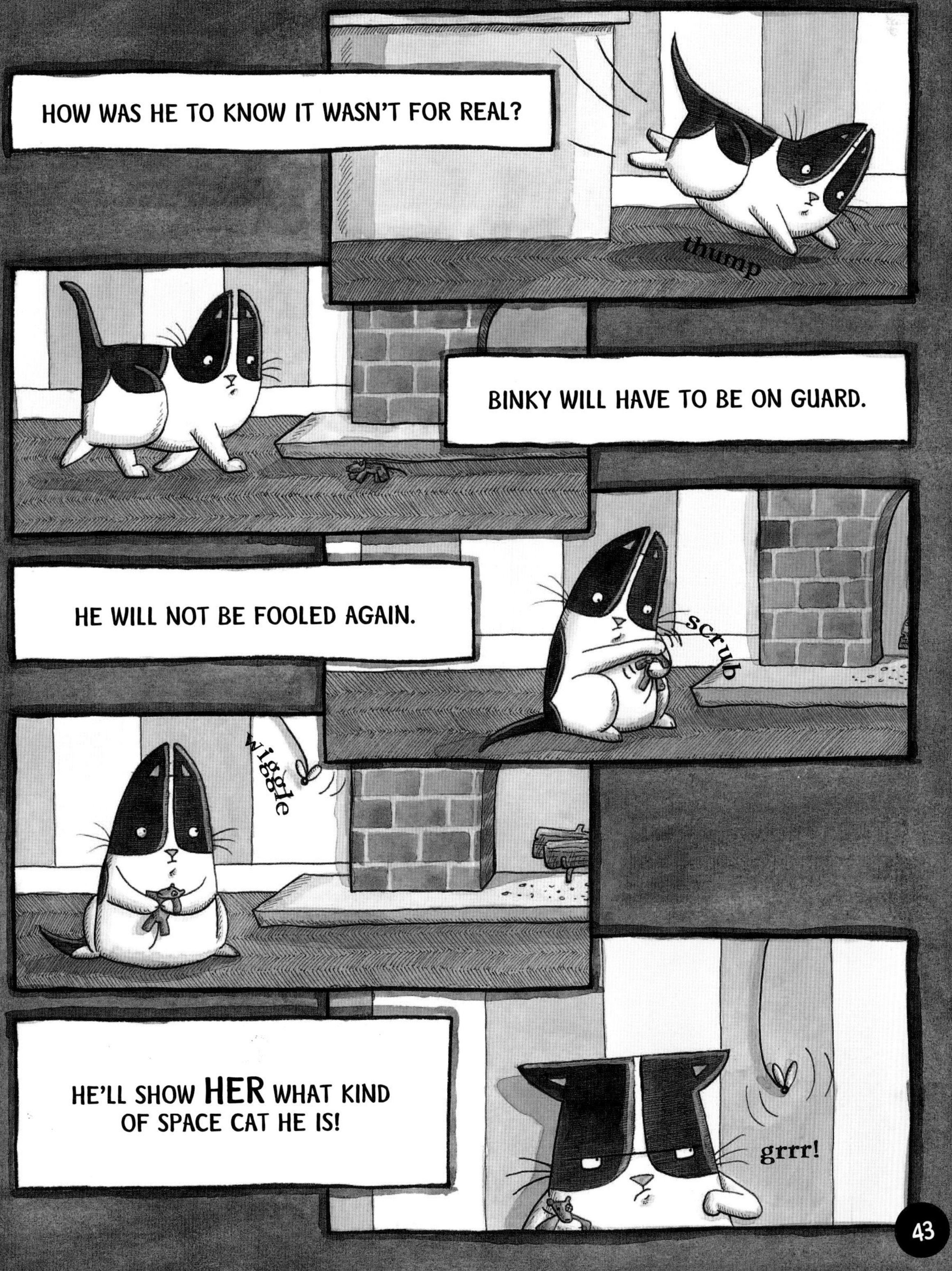
HOW WAS HE TO KNOW IT WASN'T FOR REAL?
thump
BINKY WILL HAVE TO BE ON GUARD.
HE WILL NOT BE FOOLED AGAIN.
scrub
wiggle
HE'LL SHOW HER WHAT KIND OF SPACE CAT HE IS!
grrr!

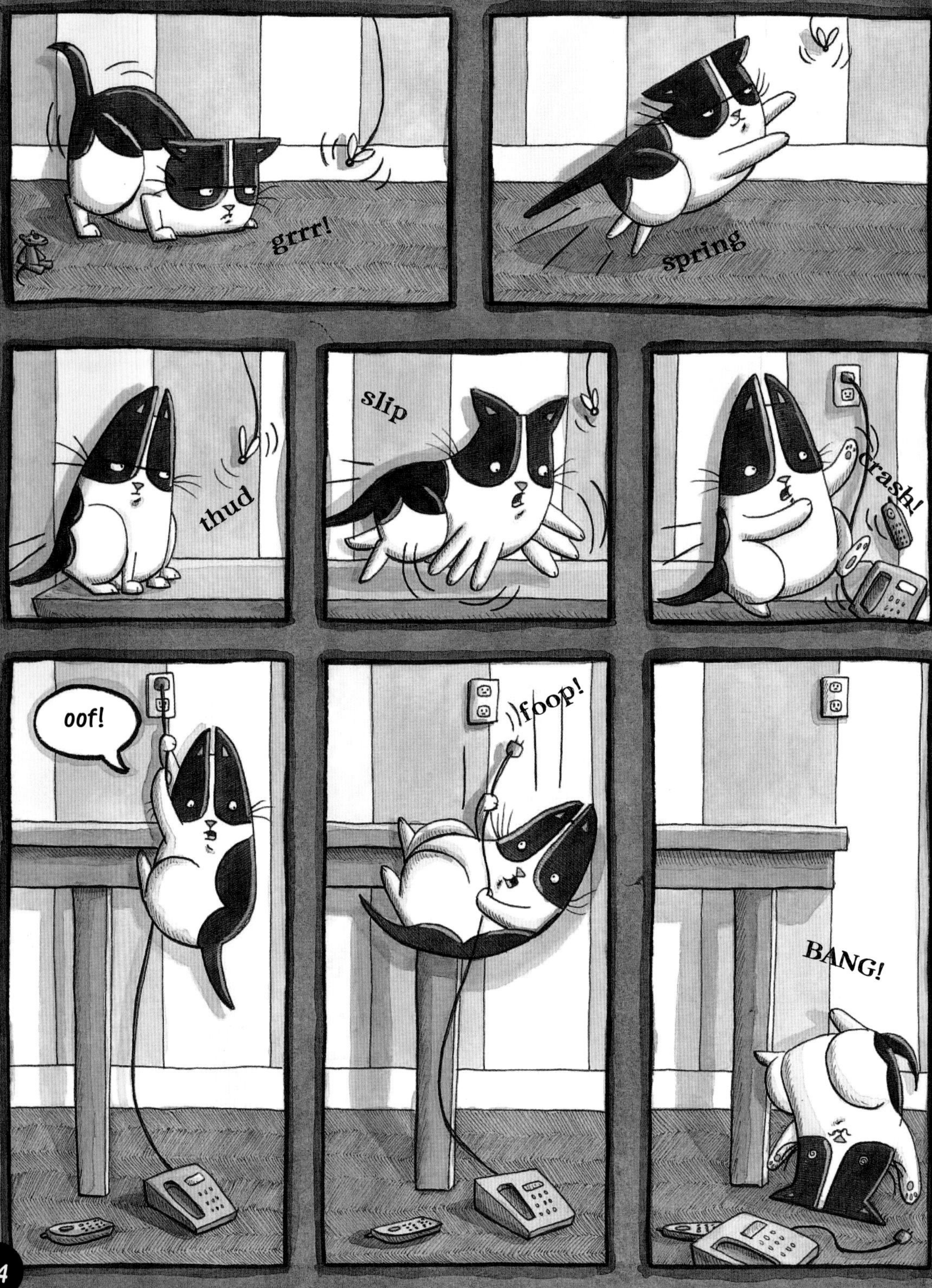
grrr!
spring
thud
slip
crash!
oof!
foop!
BANG!

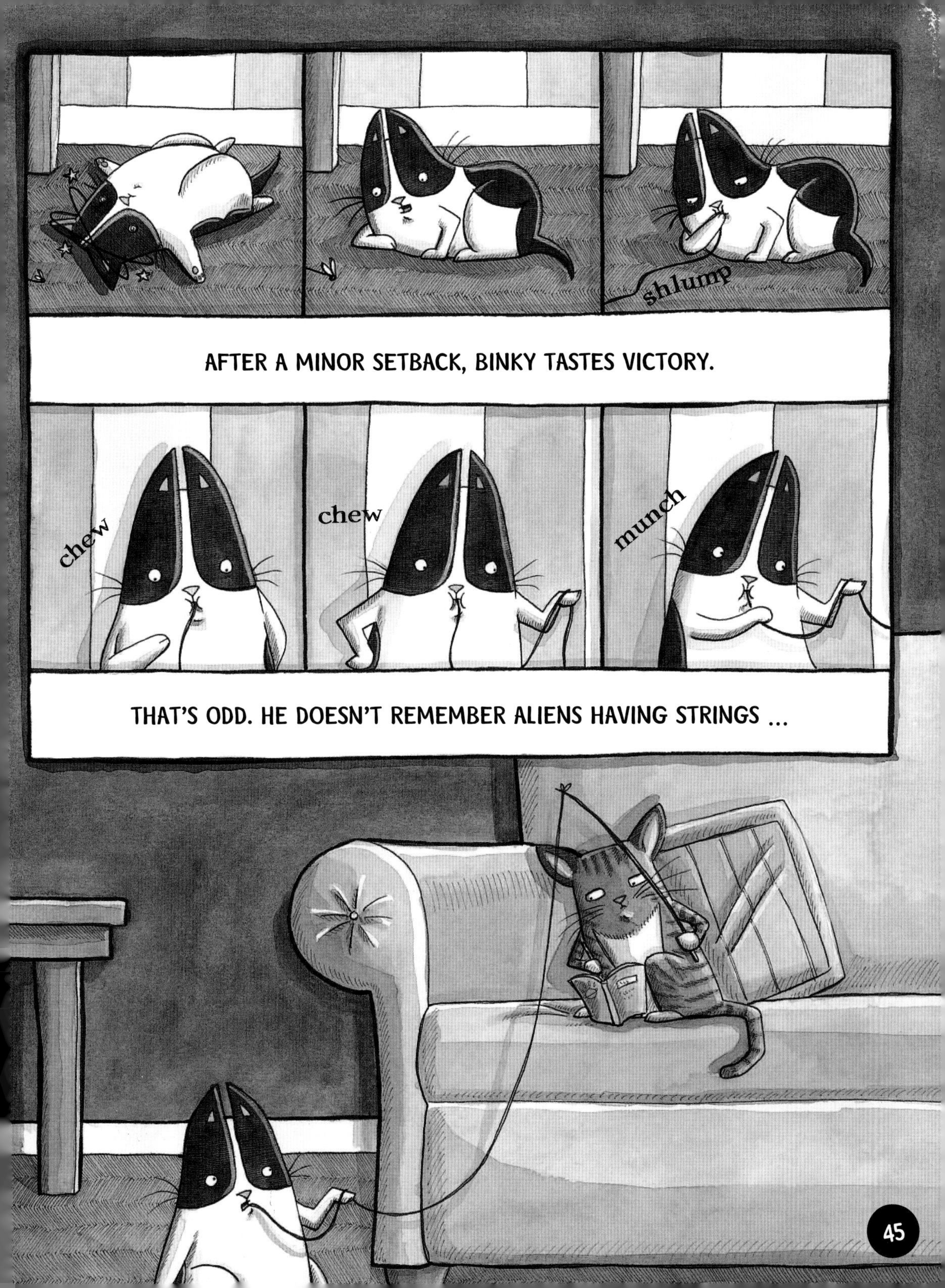

shlump
AFTER A MINOR SETBACK, BINKY TASTES VICTORY.
chew
chew
munch
THAT'S ODD. HE DOESN'T REMEMBER ALIENS HAVING STRINGS ...

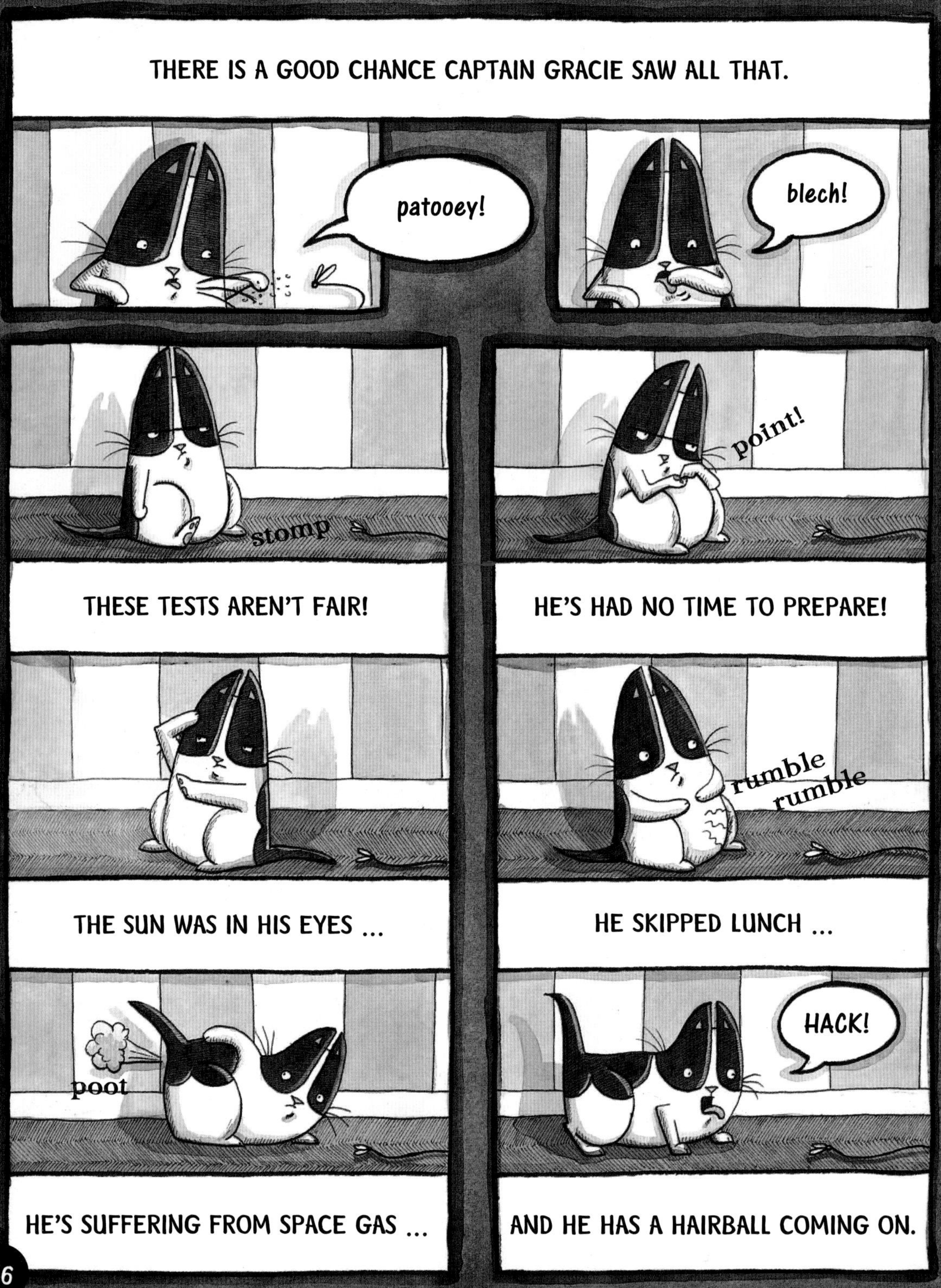
THERE IS A GOOD CHANCE CAPTAIN GRACIE SAW ALL THAT.
patooey!
blech!
stomp
point!
THESE TESTS AREN'T FAIR!
HE'S HAD NO TIME TO PREPARE!
rumble
rumble
THE SUN WAS IN HIS EYES ...
HE SKIPPED LUNCH ...
poot
HACK!
HE'S SUFFERING FROM SPACE GAS ...
AND HE HAS A HAIRBALL COMING ON.

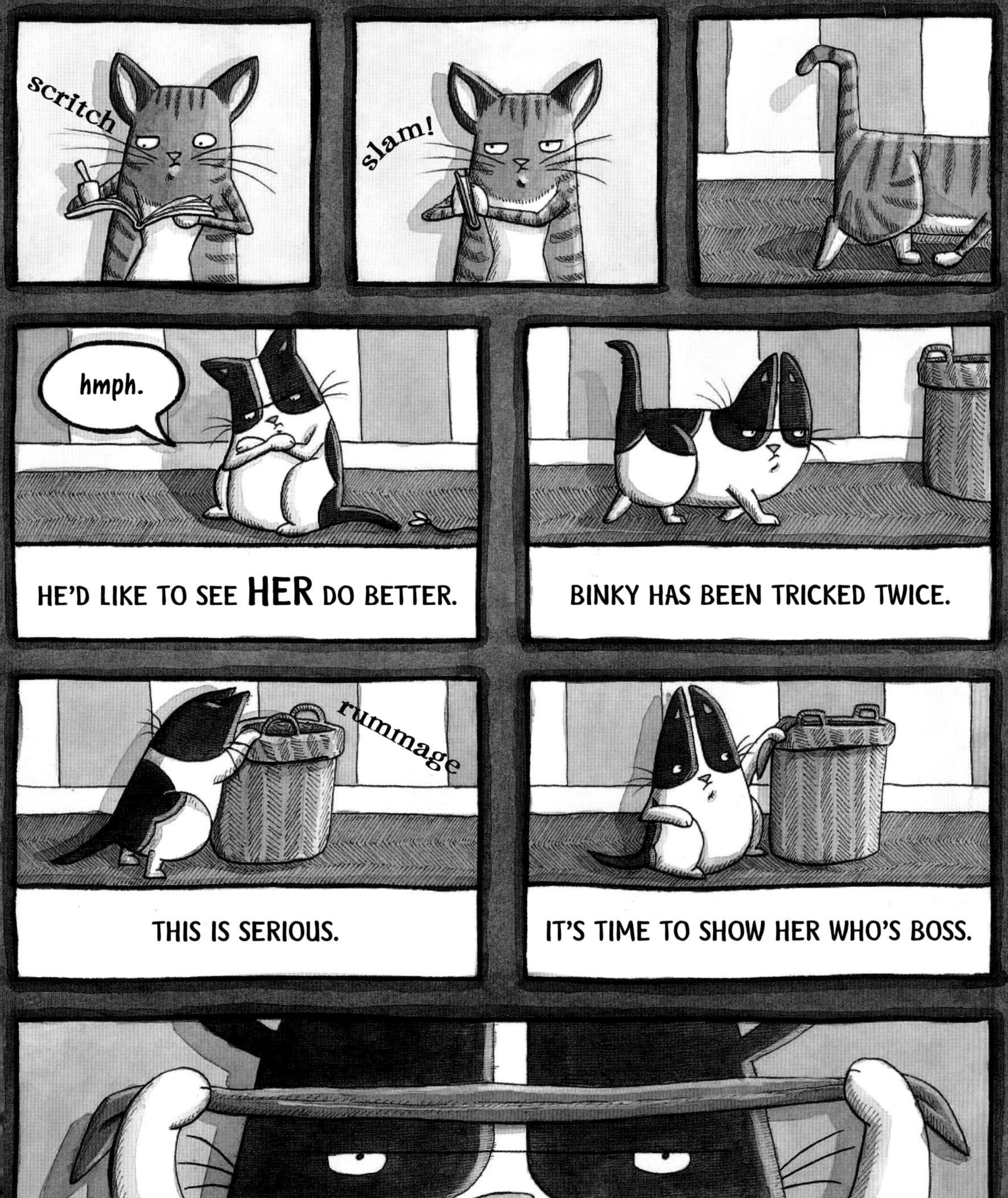
scritch
slam!
hmph.
HE'D LIKE TO SEE HER DO BETTER.
BINKY HAS BEEN TRICKED TWICE.
rummage
THIS IS SERIOUS.
IT'S TIME TO SHOW HER WHO'S BOSS.
NO MORE MR. NICE KITTY.

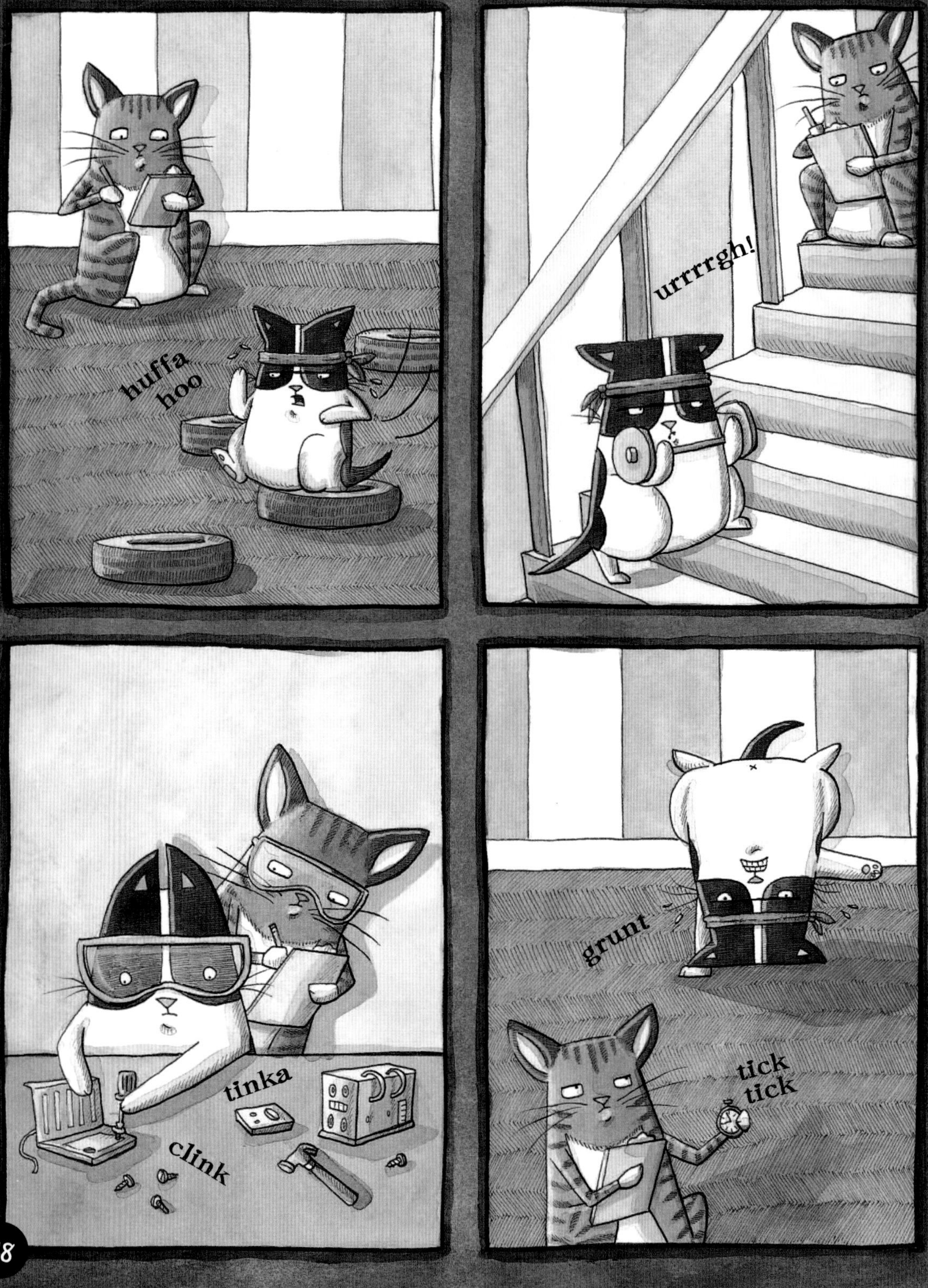
huffa
hoo
urrrrgh!
tinka
clink
grunt
tick
tick

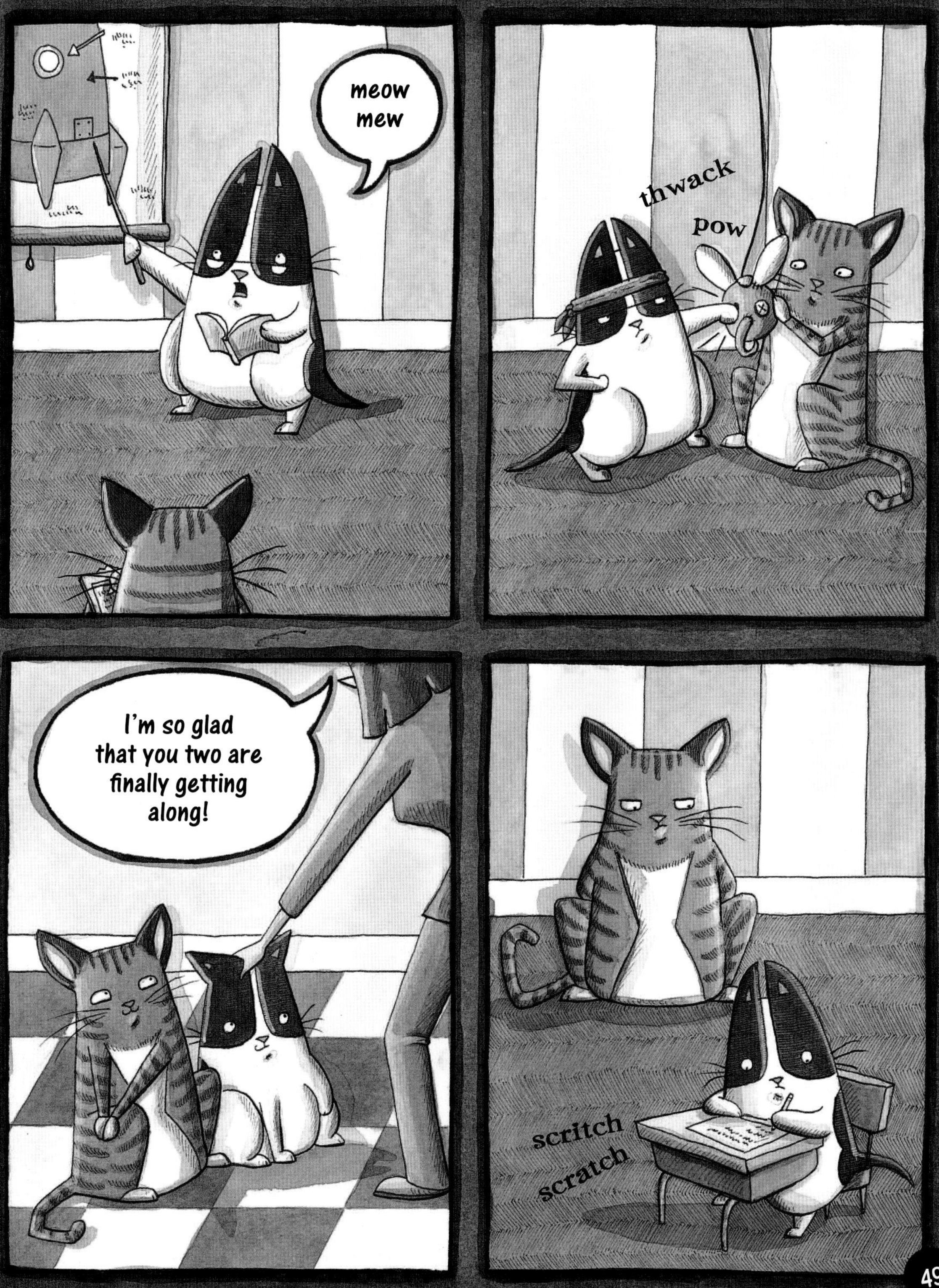
meow mew
thwack
pow
I'm so glad that you two are finally getting along!
scritch
scratch

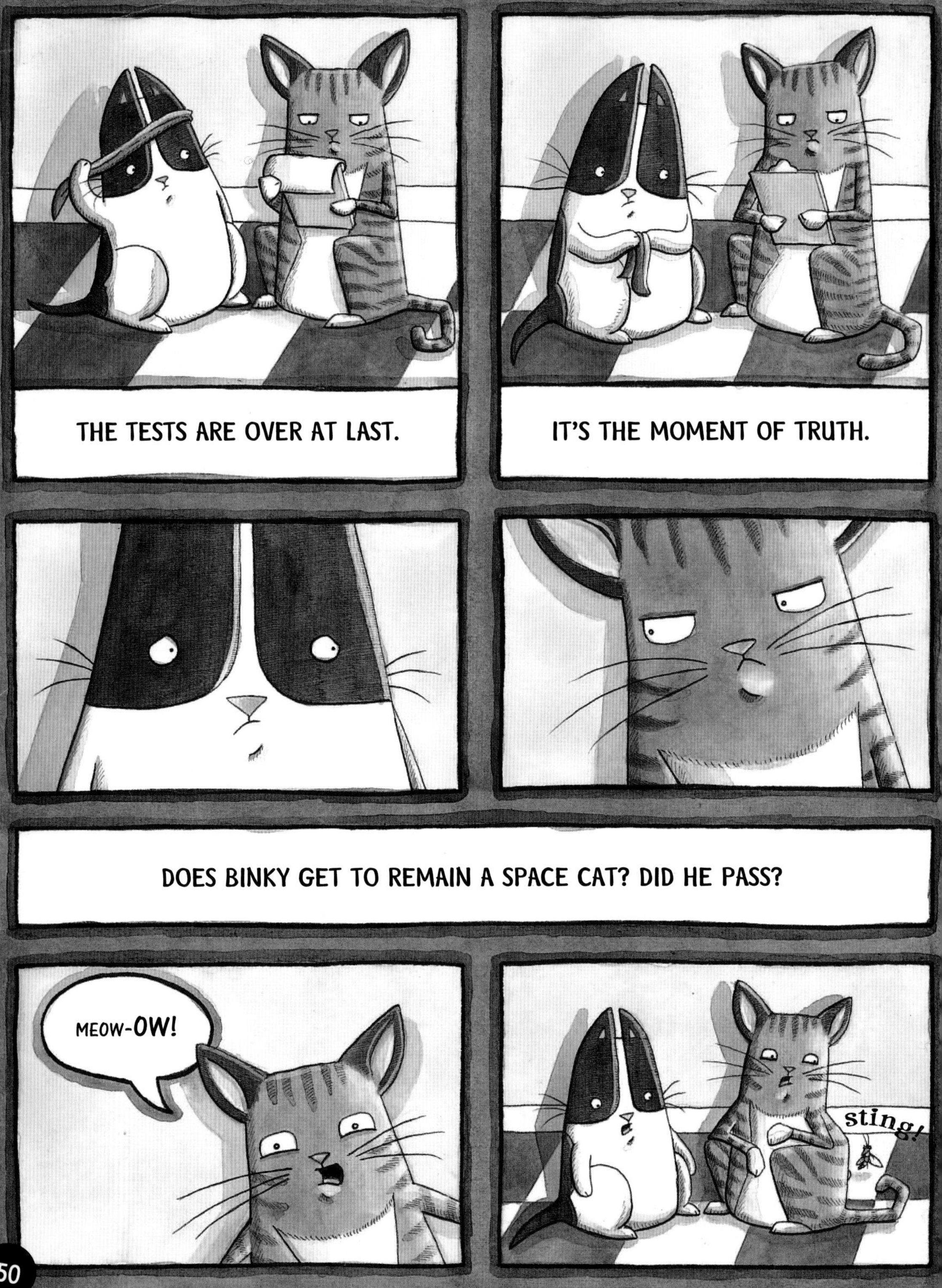
THE TESTS ARE OVER AT LAST.
IT'S THE MOMENT OF TRUTH.
DOES BINKY GET TO REMAIN A SPACE CAT? DID HE PASS?
MEOW-OW!
sting!

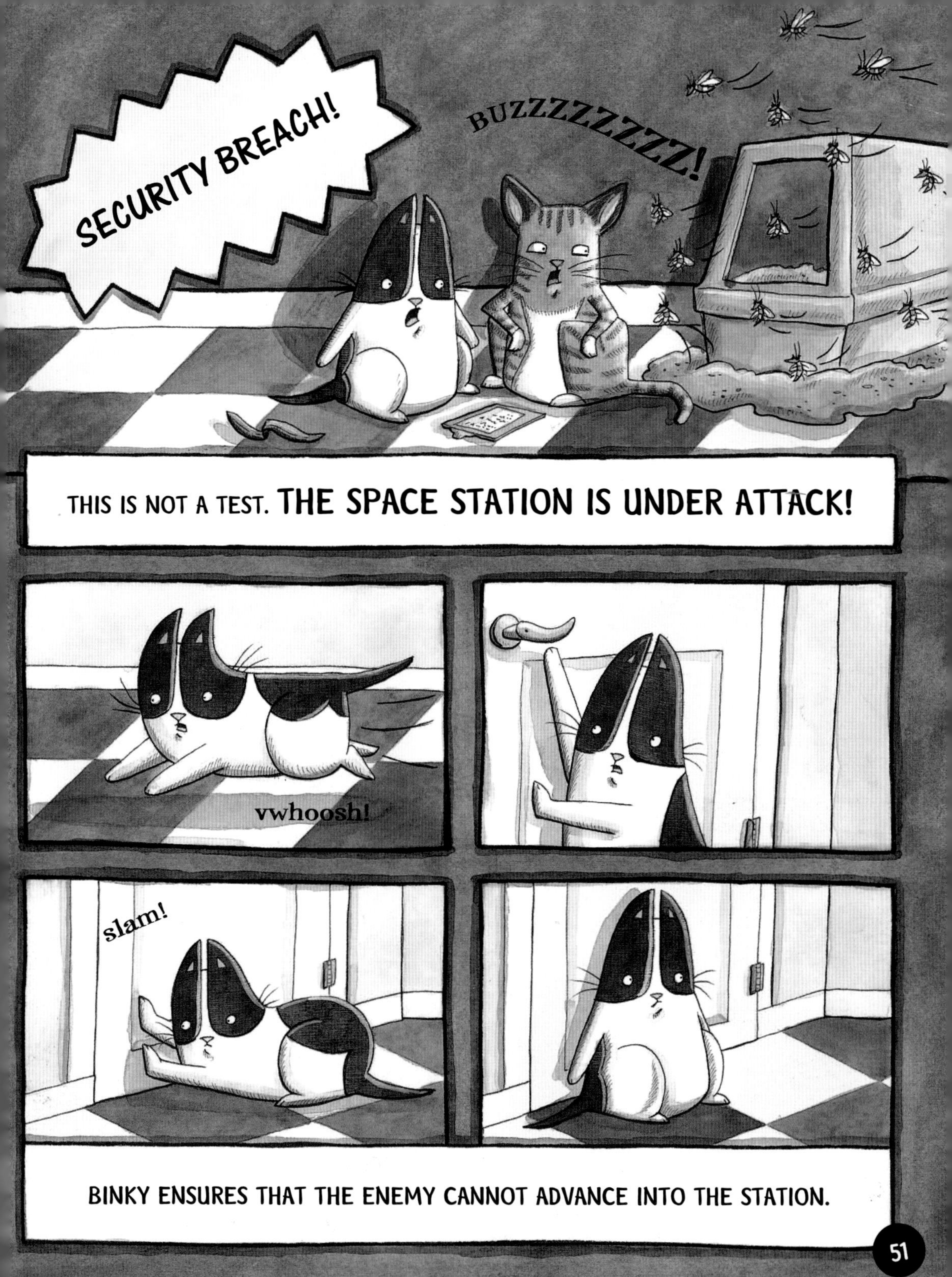
SECURITY BREACH!
BUZZZZZZZZZ!
THIS IS NOT A TEST. THE SPACE STATION IS UNDER ATTACK!
vwhoosh!
slam!
BINKY ENSURES THAT THE ENEMY CANNOT ADVANCE INTO THE STATION.

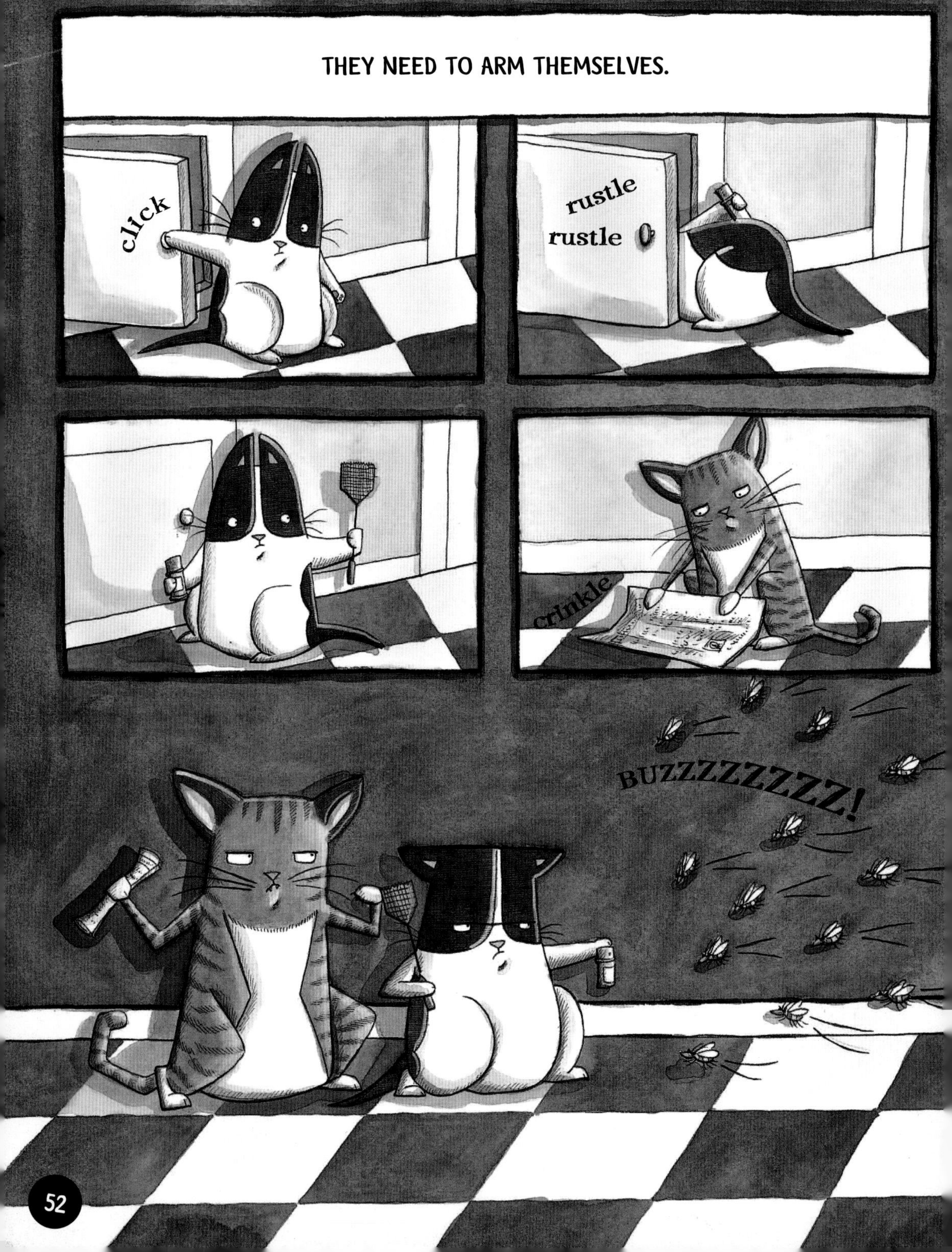

THEY NEED TO ARM THEMSELVES.
click
rustle
rustle
crinkle
BUZZZZZZZZ!

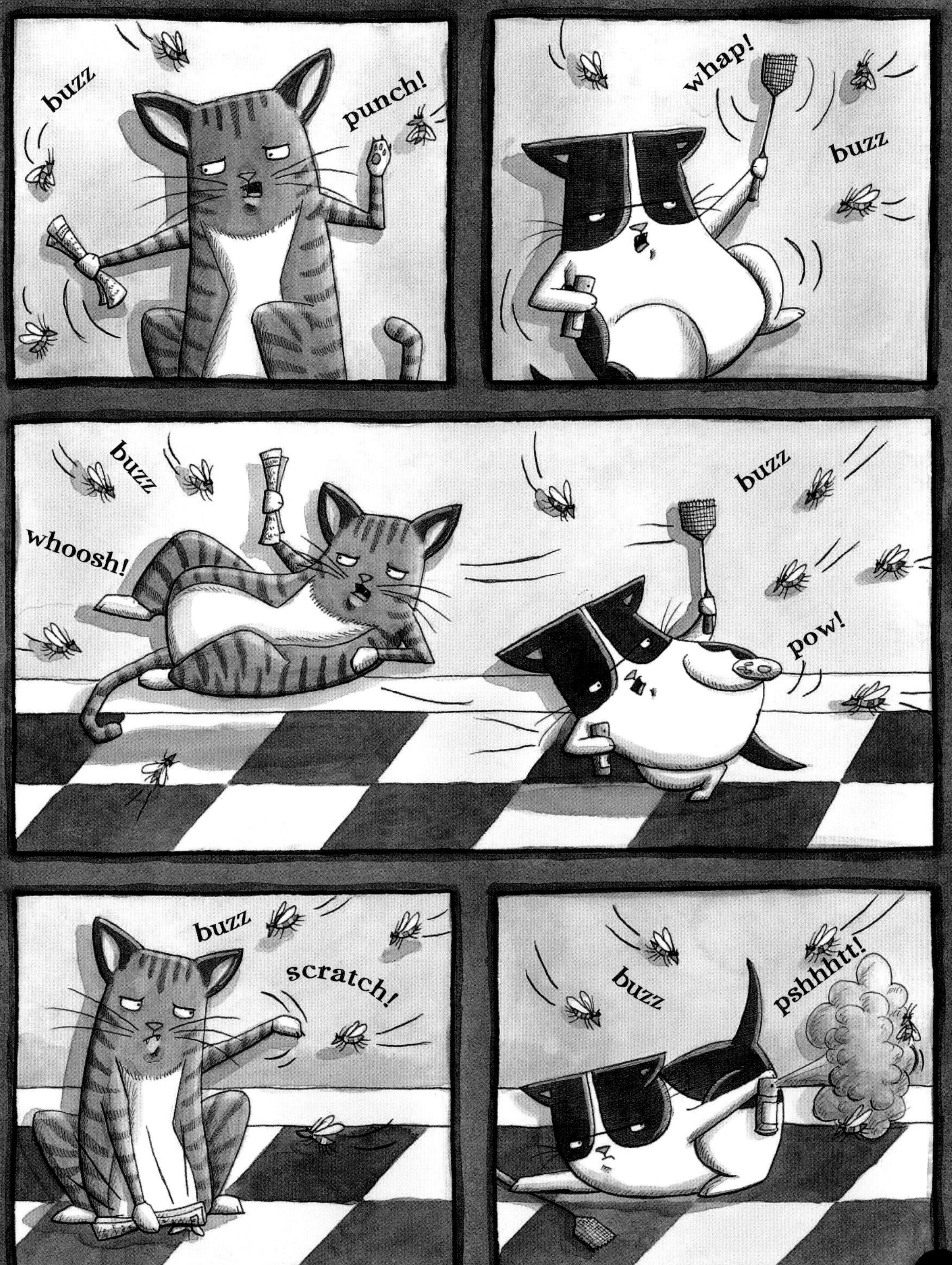
buzz
punch!
whap!
buzz
buzz
whoosh!
buzz
pow!
buzz
scratch!
buzz
pshhhtt!

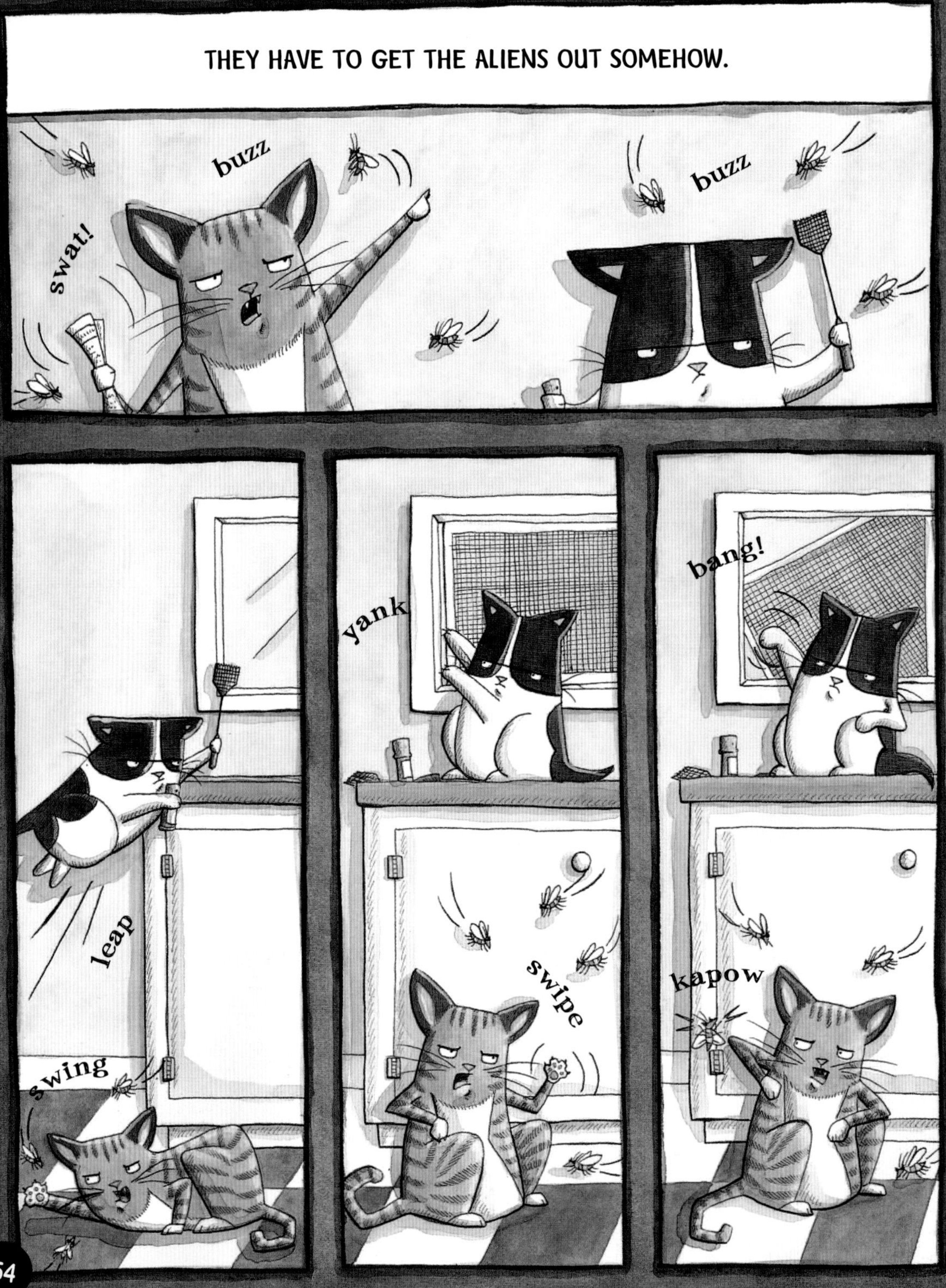
THEY HAVE TO GET THE ALIENS OUT SOMEHOW.
buzz
swat!
buzz
leap
swing
yank
swipe
bang!
kapow

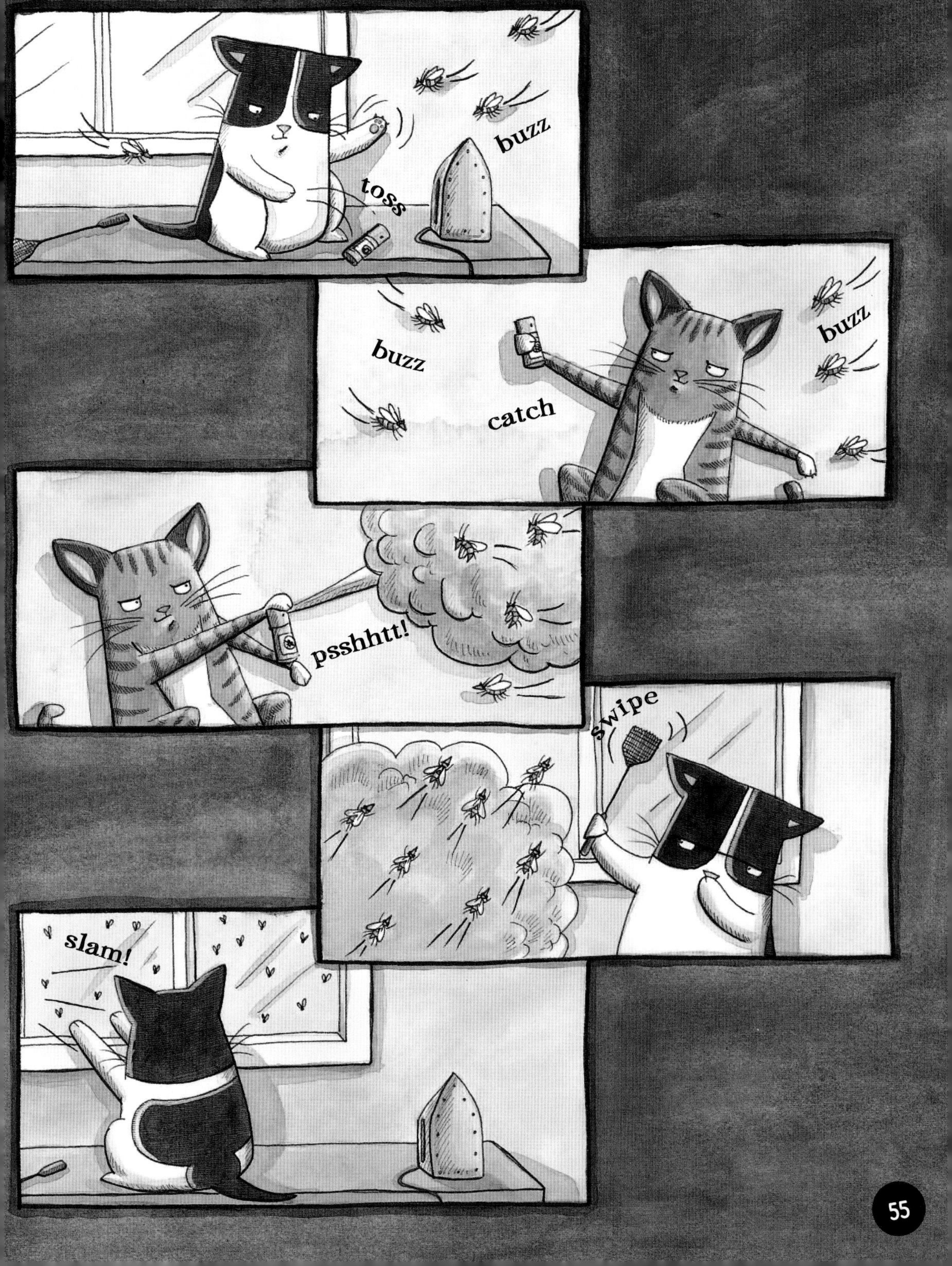
buzz
toss
buzz
buzz
catch
psshhtt!
swipe
slam!

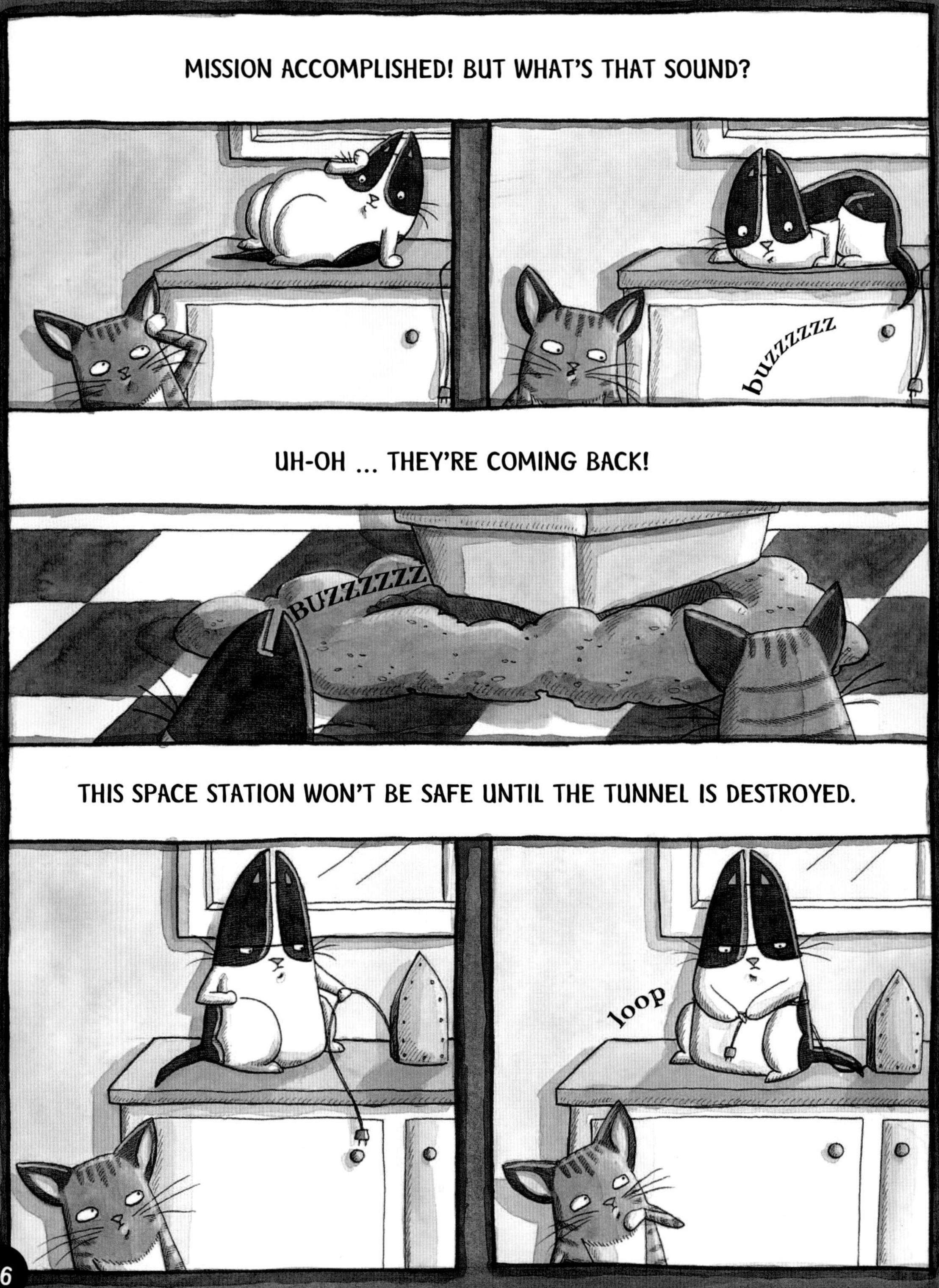
MISSION ACCOMPLISHED! BUT WHAT'S THAT SOUND?
buzzzzzz
UH-OH ... THEY'RE COMING BACK!
BUZZZZZZ
THIS SPACE STATION WON'T BE SAFE UNTIL THE TUNNEL IS DESTROYED.
loop

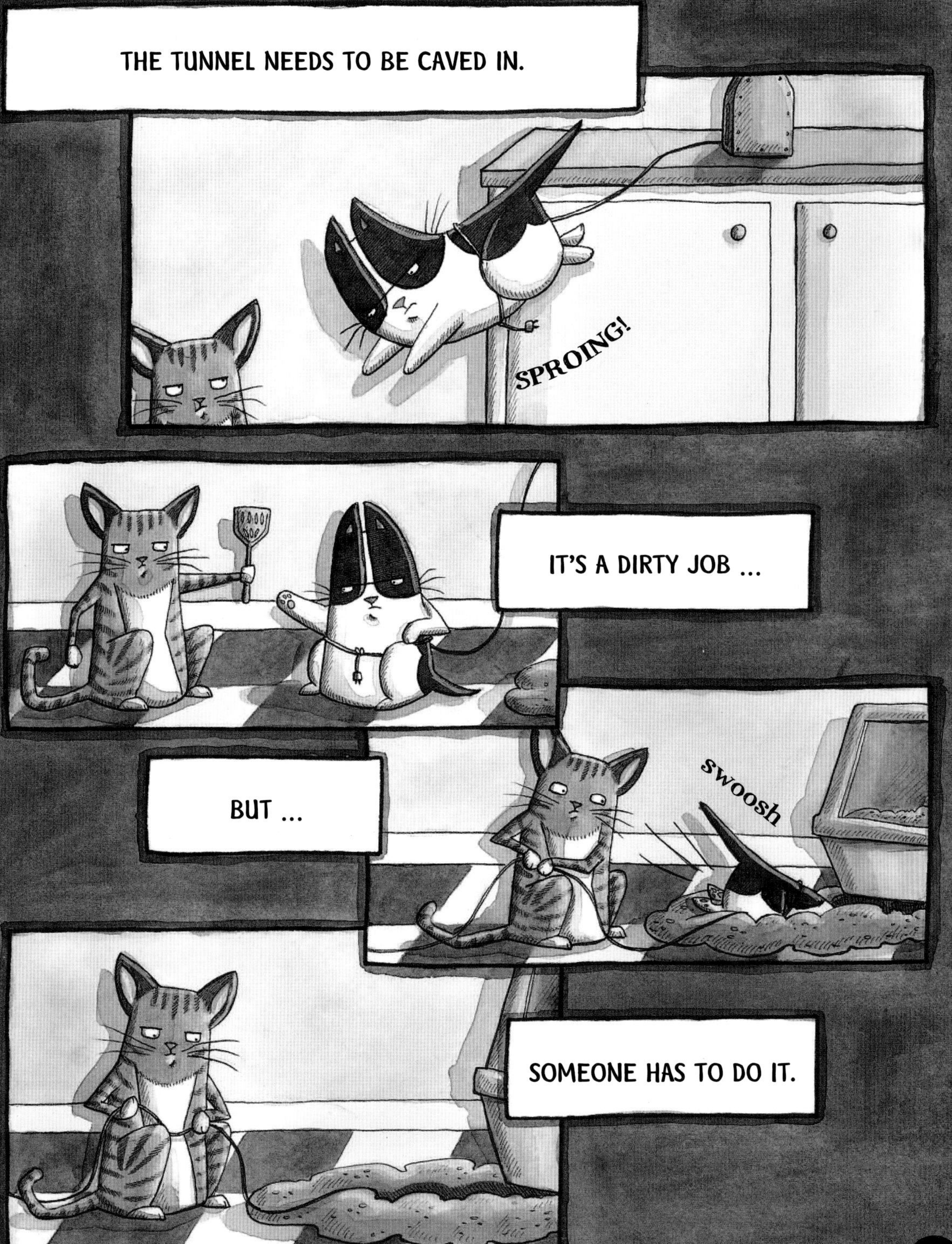
THE TUNNEL NEEDS TO BE CAVED IN.
SPROING!
IT'S A DIRTY JOB ...
BUT ...
swoosh
SOMEONE HAS TO DO IT.

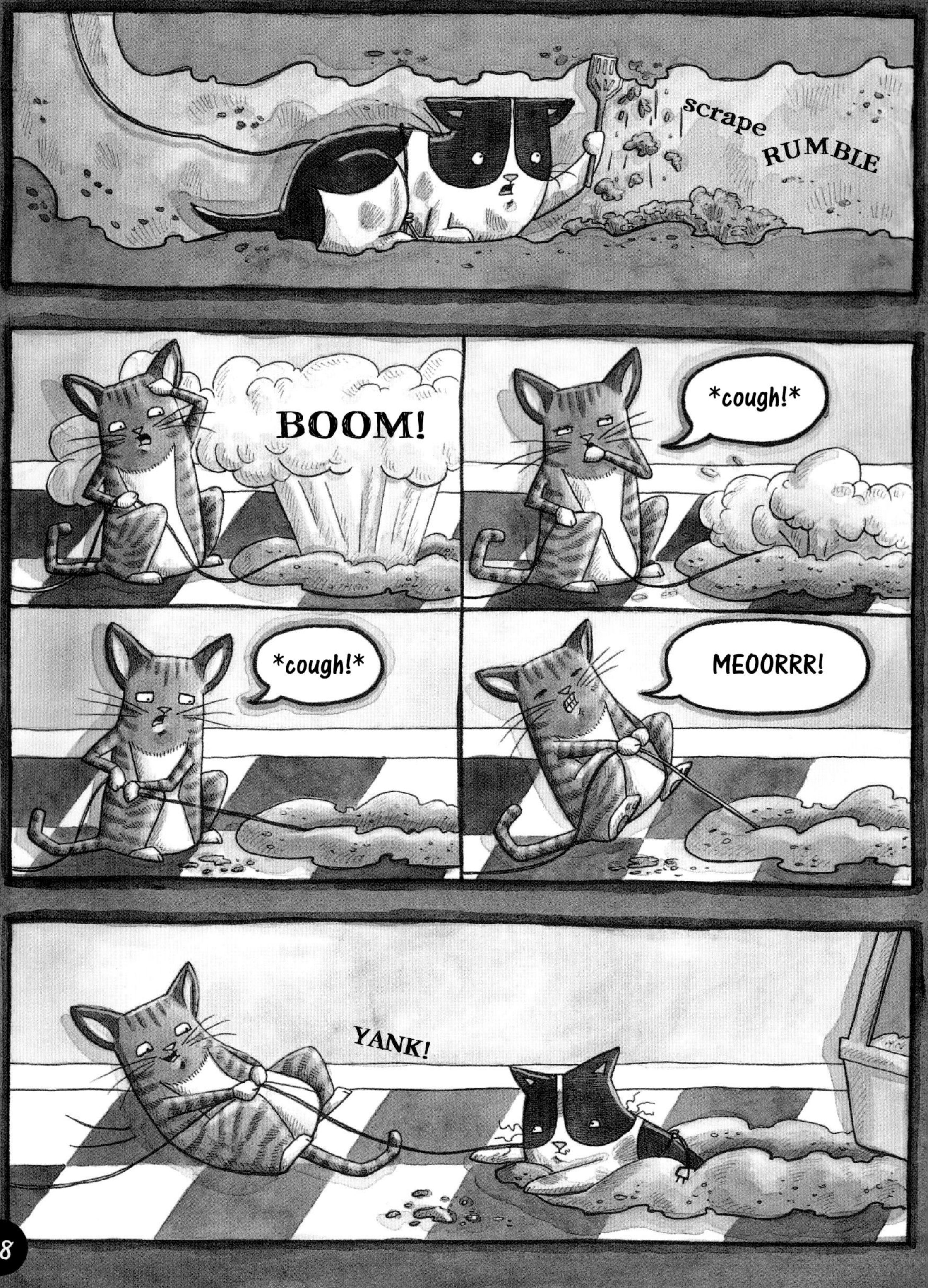
scrape
RUMBLE
BOOM!
cough!
cough!
MEOORRR!
YANK!

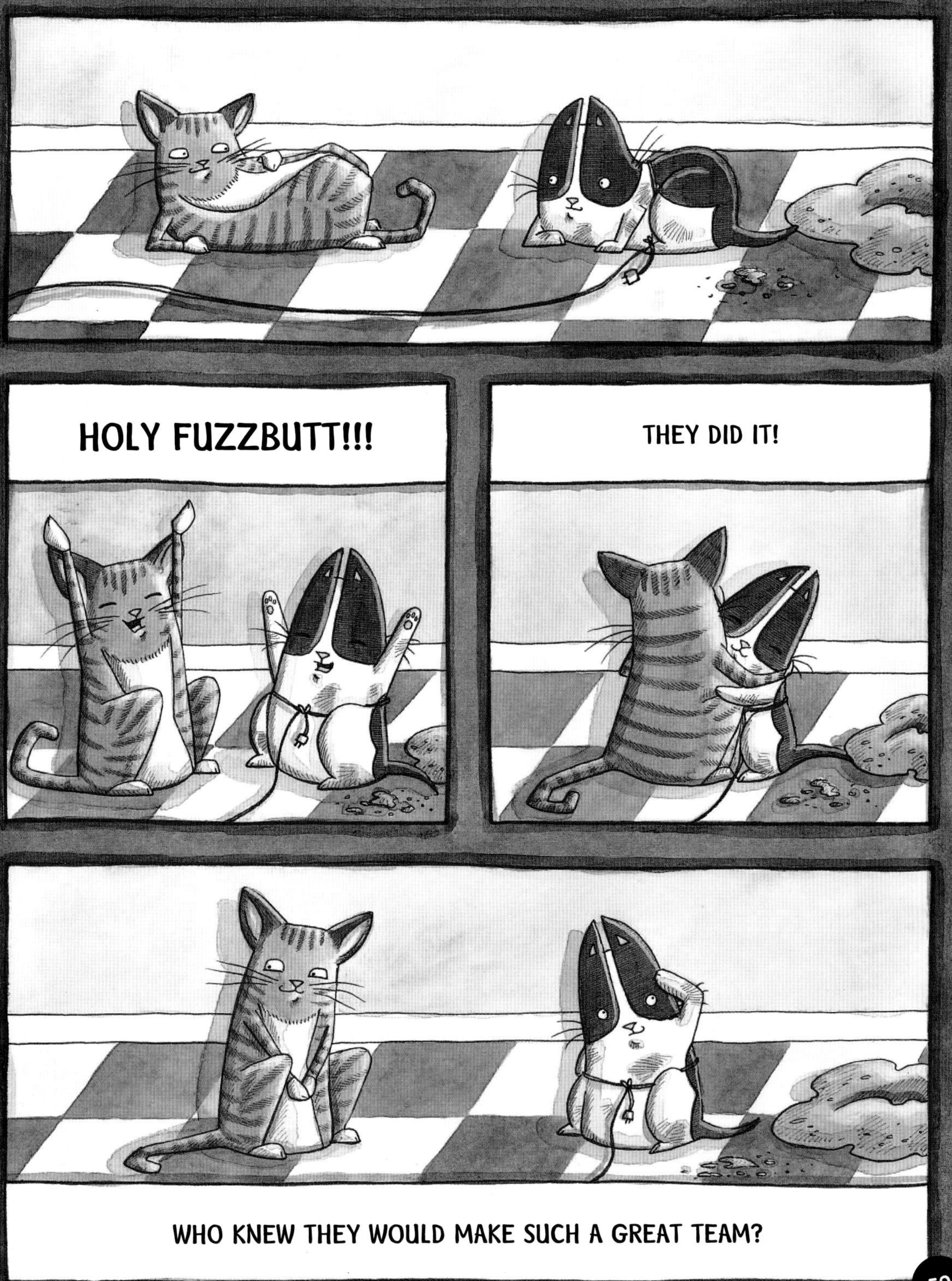
HOLY FUZZBUTT!!!
THEY DID IT!
WHO KNEW THEY WOULD MAKE SUCH A GREAT TEAM?

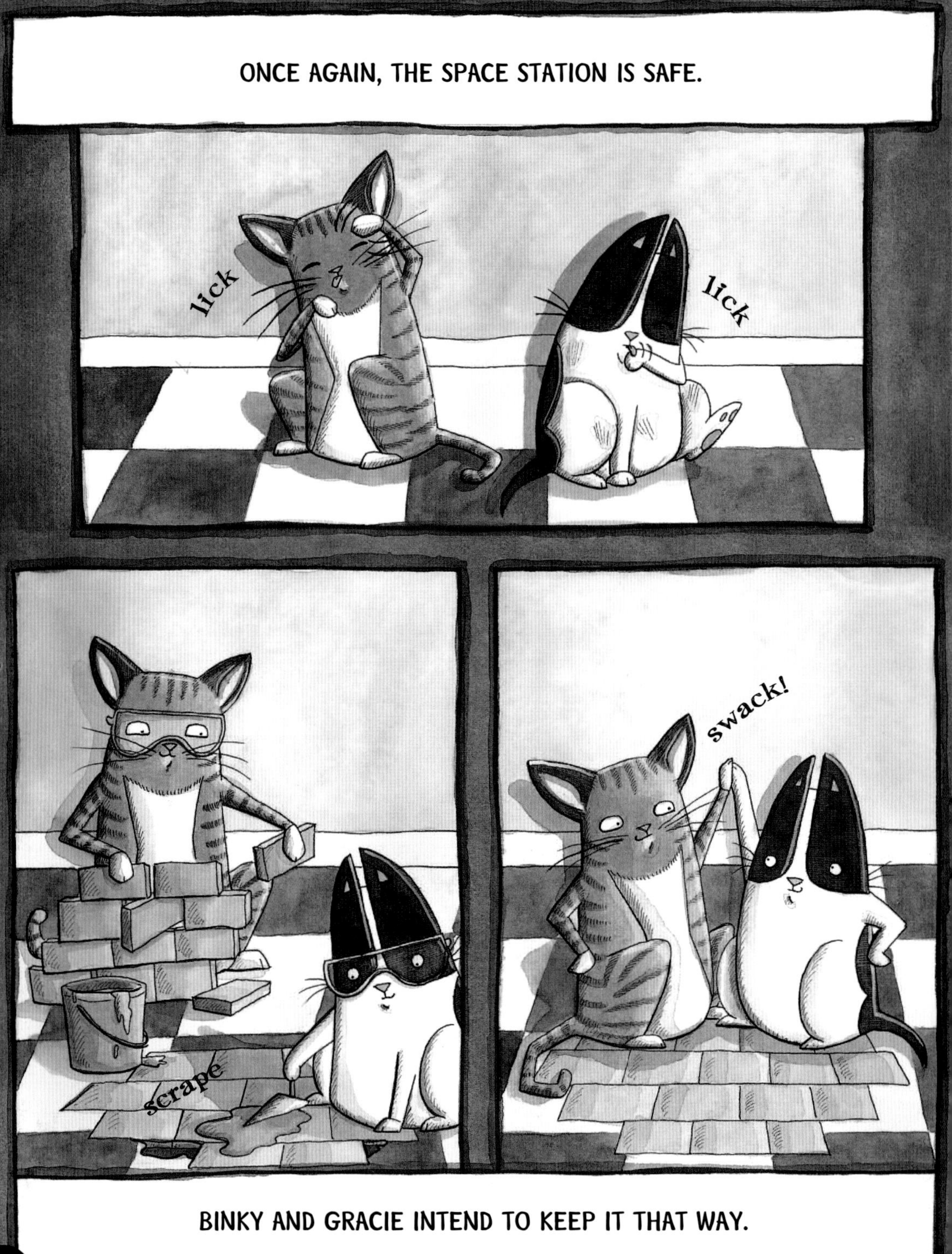
ONCE AGAIN, THE SPACE STATION IS SAFE.
lick
lick
scrape
swack!
BINKY AND GRACIE INTEND TO KEEP IT THAT WAY.

CAPTAIN GRACIE SENDS
HER REPORT
TO F.U.R.S.T.
HEADQUARTERS.

BINKY NOT ONLY REMAINS A SPACE CAT ...

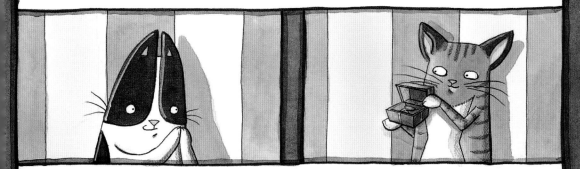

HE'S BEEN PROMOTED.

BINKY, SPACE CAT EXTRAORDINAIRE, IS BACK!!

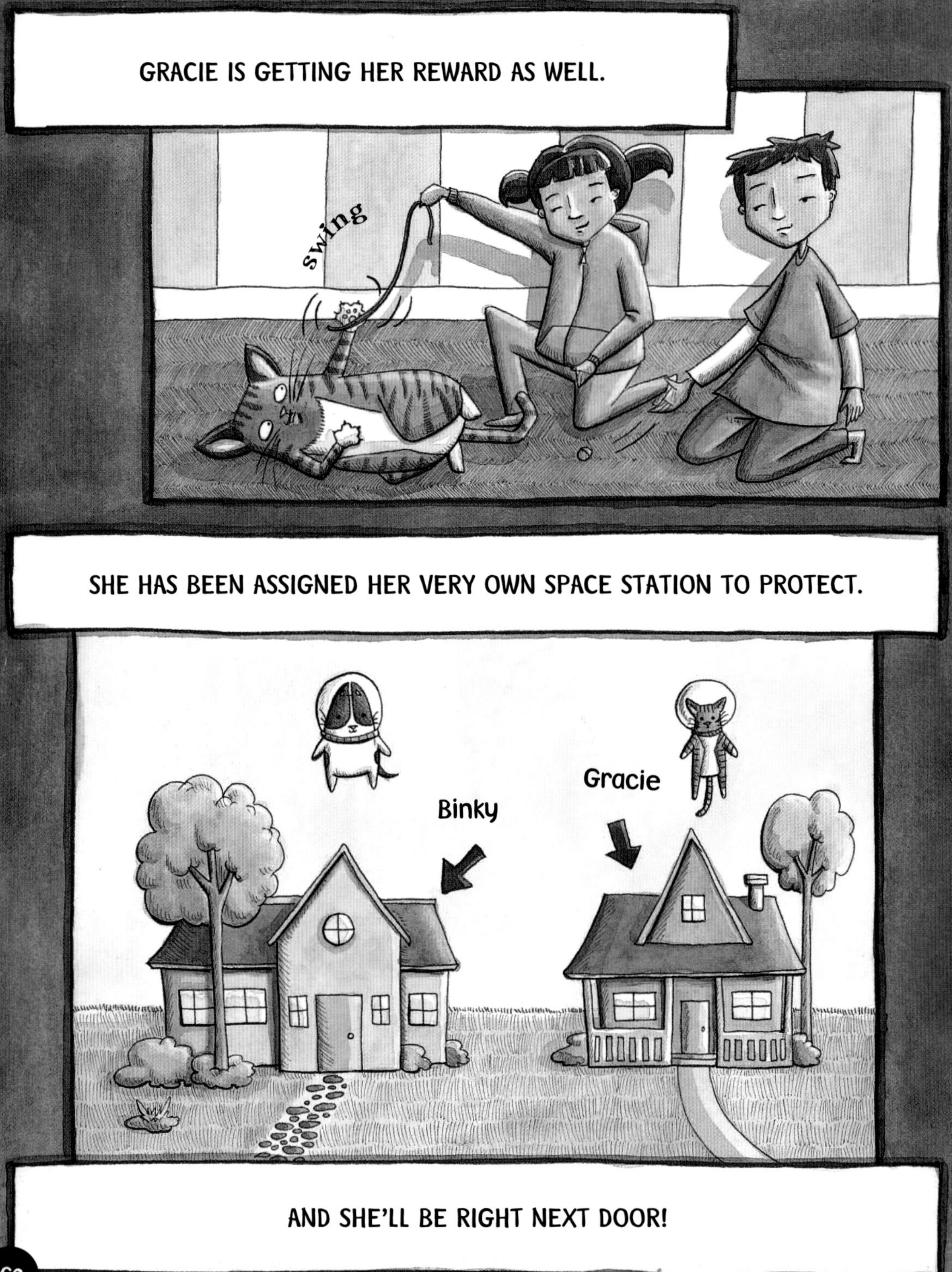
GRACIE IS GETTING HER REWARD AS WELL.
swing
SHE HAS BEEN ASSIGNED HER VERY OWN SPACE STATION TO PROTECT.
Binky
Gracie
AND SHE'LL BE RIGHT NEXT DOOR!

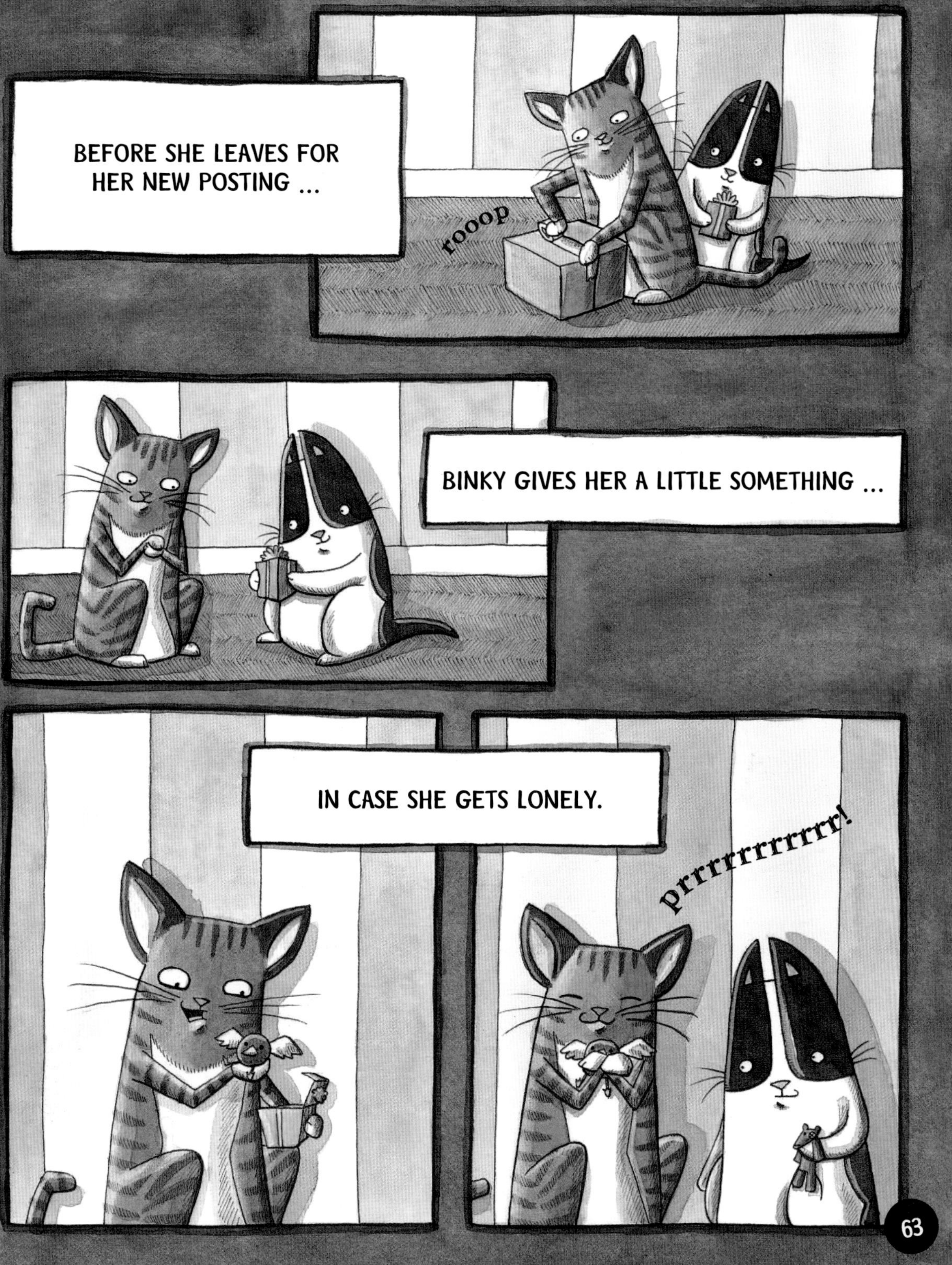
BEFORE SHE LEAVES FOR HER NEW POSTING ...
rooop
BINKY GIVES HER A LITTLE SOMETHING ...
IN CASE SHE GETS LONELY.
prrrrrrrrrr!

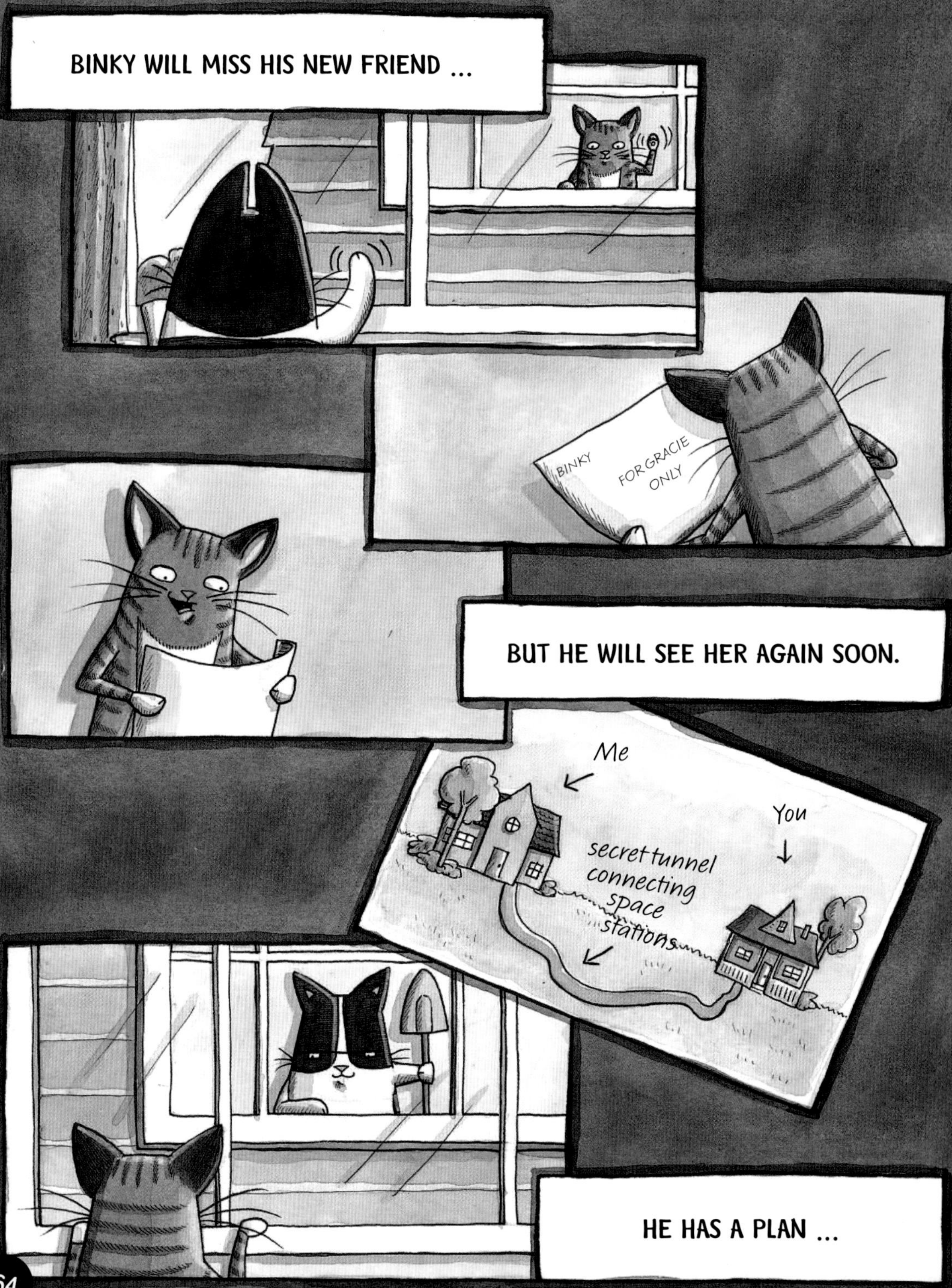
BINKY WILL MISS HIS NEW FRIEND ...
BINKY
FOR GRACIE ONLY
BUT HE WILL SEE HER AGAIN SOON.
Me
You
secret tunnel connecting space stations
HE HAS A PLAN ...